DISCARDED

The Changed Series

CHRISTINA LANIER

Discarded: The Changed Series Book 0.5
Copyright © 2021 by Christina Lanier

$\maltese$ I $\maltese$

In the year 2045

My small hand held up a dirty, naked doll, making her bounce around in the air. "And what is YOUR name," I made her ask in a high-pitched and *very* girly voice. My other hand rose in the air holding up a small, filthy teddy bear that I'd found in the nearby dumpster. He was missing an eye and an arm and almost all of his stuffing was gone but, to me, he was a wonderful find!

"My name is Baby Bear," I had the bear reply in the sweetest baby voice I could make. I'd heard a mom in a neighbor's house using the 'Baby Bear' voice, and I was pretty sure I had it right. "I'm getting ready to go to a *real* school!" I didn't really know what a real school was like because I was homeschooled, but I'd seen lots of kids getting off the bus. Since they all looked happy, I figured it had to be a pretty great place. At least, better than here anyway.

"Taryn!!! Get your lazy ass in here, you little bitch!" The screech echoed out from inside the small, single-wide trailer nearby. It startled me so bad, I dropped both of my new treasures to the dirt. My head whipped around, long, matted blonde hair flying, expecting to find *her* right behind me.

Of course, she wasn't. She never deigned to come after me and most of the time, she didn't have to. I'd learned that lesson early on. If they had to come after me, it would be *much* worse. My mind raced as I tried to remember if there was something I had forgotten to do. Fear coursed through me, making my tiny frame tremble.

Slowly, I rose to my bare feet and began to edge my way closer to the trailer. My mind was a whirlwind of frantic chaos. I had made my bed. The fear grew the closer I got to the front door. I had swept the floor even though no amount of sweeping ever really got it clean.

"Taryn!" The scream came again, making me jump in fright. "Don't make me come after you!"

No. No, I wouldn't make her come after me. That would be so, *so* bad. My pace quickened and I was at the trailer steps before I knew it. I could feel my pulse pounding in my throat. Though it wouldn't do any good, I made a quick attempt to brush the dirt from my shorts and legs before I got to the open door.

"Yes, Mama?" I called quietly, my voice quivering as I peered into the dark room beyond. I don't know why I felt the need to be quiet when she'd been screaming seconds before. Maybe I had a hope somewhere that it would encourage her to be quiet too. Or maybe I was just too scared for my voice to get any louder.

Faster than I could blink, a strong, firm hand wrapped around my upper arm, yanking me inside so hard that my head snapped back from the force. My small body flew around in a half circle before being slammed into the wall opposite the front door. *Ouchie!* A whimper escaped me as pain arched through my back, the air leaving my lungs in a *whoosh*.

Mama's red, snarling face was inches from mine. "What did I tell you?" she hissed, tightening her grip painfully on my arm.

Mama had told me a lot of things. She'd told me so much that it was hard to remember it all sometimes. I didn't know which thing she was asking me about. My blue eyes were huge in my face and I was panting from fear but I knew, if I didn't offer up some sort of answer, she'd get really mad.

"I-I-I... Y-you said...," I managed to squeak out before a growling noise escaped Mama, cutting me off from whatever else I was going to babble. Her eyes narrowed and her hand left my arm long enough to grasp the front of my threadbare t-shirt in her fist. My feet left the ground as she lifted me into the air and slammed me back into the wall again when she'd straightened to her full height. A yelp escaped me as pain raced through my back. Automatically, my hands rose to grasp her wrist.

She shook me, a look of disgust on her face that I'd shown weakness. My head thumped back onto the corner of a picture frame, causing a fresh slice of pain, but I pressed my lips together trying not to make any more noise as I willed the tears away. I couldn't help but squirm to try to get down.

Mama moved toward the small kitchen, still holding me aloft. She swung her arm toward the sink, making my short, skinny legs smack into the edge of the counter as my body moved with her motion.

"What is this?" she demanded, dropping me down to the floor so hard that my knees nearly buckled.

It took me a moment to focus on where she was pointing. *Oh, no!* There was an empty bottle and a dirty glass in the sink. But...but...I had *done* the dishes!! My eyes snapped to the dish drainer where I could clearly see the dishes I'd done this morning, still damp from being washed. I looked from the sink back up to her furious face in confusion.

A satisfied smirk tilted the edge of her mouth. I didn't know what had happened. How had I missed them? They were right there!

"Well?!" she demanded again.

"I...it's dishes," I whispered, unable to keep my lower lip from trembling. My eyes burned as the tears tried to make their appearance once again.

"Yes. It is. And you know what that means." She grabbed the back of my head and shoved it forward toward the sink. I just barely moved it enough so that it didn't bang on the faucet. Sometimes I didn't move fast enough and got a red mark from it. "Get these damn dishes done. No food for you for the rest of the day. I don't know any other six-year-old girl as stupid and lazy as you are."

Stupid. Lazy. I kept my head down as I heard her stomp back toward the living room. No food. For the rest of the day. My belly already gnawed with hunger. What was I going to do? Several tears managed to escape my eyes and rolled down my cheeks, but I quickly wiped them away. I shoved my fist into my mouth to stifle the sobs that wanted to break free. Lifting my chin, I took the empty brown bottle and threw it in the trash can before quickly washing out the glass and adding it to the dish drainer.

I listened carefully, but I didn't hear her moving nearby, so I turned and, seeing the coast was clear, made a dash for the front door. I tripped down the steps as my little legs took me as fast as they could to the woods that lined the trailer park. I snatched up my prizes on the way to the relative safety of the trees.

Most kids might be scared of being in the woods alone. Not me. I'm a big girl and I like to be in the woods by myself. There are lots of places to hide in there. If I wanted to, I could stay out here all the time and Mama would never find me.

I ducked under branches as I ran. Thorns and twigs cut into my bare feet, but I hardly noticed in my rush to get away. Soon, all I could hear were birds chirping and the faint rustling of small animals as they moved around the forest. I saw a familiar fallen tree trunk with one end almost completely covered with branches. I scampered over to it and slid in, hiding among the cage of branches and leaves. My heart was pounding furiously in my chest as I sat as still and quietly as possible, listening to see if she decided to come after me. My back was aching and it hurt to move around too much. My head hurt too. There was a sharp pain where I hit the picture frame and when I reached up to touch it, my fingers came away bloody. Quickly, I wiped it off on my dirty shorts. I don't like blood even though I see it a lot.

It seemed like *ages* that I sat there, still and listening. Finally, almost scared it was a trick, I peeked my head out and looked all around for her. I didn't see her anywhere. Heaving a big sigh, I sat back down with my new friends.

"This is *your* fault," I said sternly to Baby Bear. I gave him a little shake, like Mama did to me. The words came, to call him lazy and stupid. Even though I don't really know what lazy means, I *do* know what stupid means and, looking at my new friend with his missing arm and lost stuffing, I couldn't say it. He might just be a stuffed animal but he's my new best friend and I didn't want him to feel like I did.

Squeezing him close to my chest in a giant hug, I whispered, "I'm sorry. You're not stupid."

The rumble of a bus sounded in the distance and I perked up, realizing the neighborhood kids were getting home from school. Mama said I couldn't play with them, but I liked to watch them anyway. They looked like they have lots of fun. I wondered, not for the first time, as I scampered back toward the edge of the tree line, if *their* Mamas made them sad.

I didn't think so, because when they got off the bus, some of them ran to their Mamas and hugged them tight. I couldn't remember Mama ever hugging me. Then again, I didn't think I'd want her to. She'd probably make it hurt. The kids laughed as they got off the bus. A small group of four boys and two girls started chasing each other nearby. They looked around my size.

As I watched, one of the boys tapped one of the girls on the arm and yelled, "Tag!", before running away. The girl laughed and started chasing the other kids. I smiled at the fun they seemed to be having. Maybe they would let me play with them! I'd always been too scared to ask, but maybe...I looked toward our trailer to make sure Mama wasn't out. The front door was closed. Butterflies danced in my tummy as I decided to see if I could play.

When one of the girls got closer to the tree line, I ran out from my hiding spot. I tapped her on the shoulder and yelled, "Tag!" just as I'd seen the boy do. But the girl didn't laugh and run. She stopped and stared at me. Then she started backing away. The other kids had stopped too and crowded around her to stare at me. Up close, they seemed a good bit bigger than me. I had to look up to see the weird looks on their faces.

That was when I started to think something was wrong. Why were they staring at me? Why weren't they playing anymore? Did I yell the wrong word?

"What is it?" one of the boys asked. He edged closer and poked at me with one finger. I stepped back, not sure if he was going to 'tag' me or try to hurt me like Mama.

"Duh," said the first girl I'd seen get tagged, "It's a kid."

"What happened to your clothes?" another boy asked.

My clothes? I looked down at myself then at each of them, trying to see what he was talking about. It only took me a moment to see the difference. My clothes were very thin, dirty, and had holes in them. Their clothes were bright, colorful, and...*not* dirty.

"Why is your hair so yucky?" the other girl asked. She didn't sound like she was saying it in a mean way. More like a sad way.

Automatically, my hand flew up to the tangled, matted blonde mass on top of my head while I looked at her hair. It looked very pretty with twists and bows in it. By this point, I was getting very uncomfortable.

Impatiently, another boy stepped forward to look me over. One hand flew to his nose and he jumped backwards. "Gross! It stinks! Don't you take a bath?"

Of course I took a shower! I took one once a week because that's when Mama said she could afford the water for me to take one. It was super cold, so I didn't stay in there long, but I *did* take a shower. They...weren't nearly as dirty as I was. My brows furrowed as I considered that. Did they take a longer time washing in their weekly showers? How could they stand the cold water?

"Hey, Adam! Isn't that your baby brother's old teddy bear?" the first girl asked, pointing to Baby Bear. "Didn't you throw it in the trash?"

They all started looking at me differently then. Their noses scrunched up and I heard somebody say, "Gross."

That wasn't nice! I'm not gross! The butterflies had gone and left a sick feeling in the pit of my belly. Before I had a chance to say anything, the same boy turned back toward the others. "Let's go to my house! My mom's getting pizza for dinner."

That sounded yummy and exciting! Maybe if I ate some pizza, the sick feeling would go away. I'd never had pizza before. What a treat! As they all moved toward one of the nicer looking trailers, I took a step toward it, too, thinking he was talking to all of us.

"Not you," the boy said, catching my movement. I froze in place. "My mom doesn't like us to bring trash in the house."

He must be talking about Baby Bear. They knew I'd gotten him out of the big trash can by the side of the road. Carefully, I leaned down and placed my two treasures on the ground. I could leave them there long enough to go try pizza. Mama and Daddy had some before and it always smelled so good, but they wouldn't let me have any. I could come back for my treasures later.

"No!" the boy said sharply. "You can't come."

"Why?" I asked quietly. I didn't understand. I would leave my treasures so they wouldn't be in his house.

"Because you look and smell like trash," he said before running away to join the other kids. The girl with ribbons gave me one last look just as they all disappeared around the side of one of the trailers.

I stayed there, frozen in place as his words sunk in. He was calling *me* trash. My bottom lip trembled, and my eyes burned with a rush of tears. I was used to hearing mean stuff from Mama and that always made me sad. Hearing it from another kid made me really, *really* sad. Because they looked so happy and fun. I didn't know happy and fun could also be mean.

I sniffled and stood up, swiping at my nose with my arm. They thought I was trash because of my treasures. I *had* gotten them out of the big green trash can. I squeezed my eyes shut tight, trying to be a big girl, but the tears managed to slide through. I didn't want people to be mean because I got my friends from the trash can. Turning away with sobs wracking my thin shoulders, I ran back into the woods, leaving my treasures in the dirt.

❦ 2 ❦

"You...you stupid...stupid...*lazy*!" I whisper-yelled to myself as I kicked my hiding log. But not too hard because I'd done that before and it had hurt! And not too loud either. If I was too loud, Mama might hear me. Already, I wanted to go back for my treasures. I was torn. I wanted them, but I didn't want people to be mean to me either. It was different when it was just Mama being mean. Now kids were being mean, too. Maybe I really *was* a stupid lazy.

The sweet sound of birds chirping seemed to change. It wasn't sweet anymore. In fact, it almost sounded like the birds were laughing at me!

Caw! Caw! Why did that sound so much like 'Ha! Ha!'?

"Shut up!" I whispered at them, looking up into the canopy of trees. Birds didn't get to be mean to me too! Suddenly, my safe place didn't seem as good as it used to be. As if that wasn't bad enough, it started to rain. Cold, fat droplets fell from the leaves overhead, plopping onto my upturned face. More and more began to fall, the drops seeming to get bigger with each one.

A small yelp escaped me as the rain suddenly came pouring down. I turned and ran back through the woods, pumping my little legs as quickly as I could while avoiding the fallen limbs and branches that covered the ground. The cold wetness easily soaked my thin shirt. The raindrops slid down the bare skin of my arms and legs, leaving goosebumps behind.

I'd been hot before, but now I was starting to shiver. Where could I go? Usually, I would go under the trailer, but last time, I had seen a snake in there, and it was one with a pointy head. I know those are the ones that can make me sick, so I don't want to go back under there. Of course, Mama wouldn't want me going in the house, but she *really* wouldn't want me going in the house wet and muddy...wet and muddy! In my rush to find some-where to hide from the rain, I'd nearly forgotten my treasures!! They were going to get muddy and there would be no one to clean them off!

Thinking about my treasures getting all dirty and sad made me turn around. Maybe I could just hide my treasures from the other kids. Then-

"Taaaaarynnnn!!!!!"

Mama!! Oh no!

I gasped, flinched, and tripped over a big branch that I was just getting ready to jump over. My foot tangled in the small branches and down I went. I crashed to the ground, getting a mouthful of leaves and dirt, but I didn't pay that any attention because I was busy looking for Mama. I pushed my hands against the dirt so that my head was high enough to peer over the branches and leaves on the ground as I looked around, sniffing carefully for that funny smell that was always around Mama.

Had she found me? That yell did *not* sound happy at all. Fear and worry raced through me. That was the way she sounded just before she did something really bad. I knew it was gonna be bad. If I didn't go straight home right *now*, I was going to hurt a lot tonight.

I didn't see her anywhere, which made my shaking ease a

little bit. She hadn't come after me. Trembling from the cold rain, that still poured down on me, and fear, I rose slowly into a crouch, looking back the way I had come. Back toward my treasures.

"Ta-*ryn*!" A deeper bellow sounded through the woods. This voice was closer, like it was at the edge of the woods and not back at the house like Mama. I ducked down again. What Mama did was nothing compared to Daddy. He was home from work! Oh, no! How did I let this happen?? He was going to be so angry. He wasn't supposed to be home yet!

My trembling increased and my teeth began to chatter. My eyes darted in the direction of home. In the distance, barely visible through the leaves and branches, I could see the large shape of a man moving on the other side of the tree line. I ducked back down as fast as I could.

I was gonna be in so much trouble! My thumb was at my mouth and I was nervously chewing on the nail before I even thought about it.

"No, stupid!" I whispered quietly to myself. "Only stupid lazies bite their nails." I didn't know if that was true or not. I only knew that was what Mama said.

"Ta-*ryn*!" That bellow was a little further away. Maybe he was going back home. I waited several long minutes before I lifted my head back up, peeking over to where I'd seen him.

He wasn't there! Carefully, I took a step backward, staying low to the ground. My eyes moved back and forth in front of me in case I missed him. Daddy was tricky sometimes. And a really good hider. I backed up a few more steps, still watching, but there was nothing. No movement at all.

I relaxed some. He went home! That was good, even if it meant he was gonna be super mad that I didn't come when he called me. It would be okay. He'd be super mad, but I'd have my treasures.

Something hard clamped onto my shoulder and I was spun

roughly around. A shriek of fear ripped from my throat but I pressed my lips tight together, cutting off the noise.

"There you are, you little bitch! Did you think you could hide from me?" Daddy's red face was twisted and angry. Drops of rain rolled down his forehead, dripping from his nose. His fingers bit painfully into my shoulder.

I stared up at him, wide-eyed and speechless, as it felt like all the blood left my face. His eyes took in my small, soaked and shaking frame. He sneered, giving me a disgusted look. I knew what that was because I'd seen families make that face when I peeked through their windows on nights when Daddy locked me outside. They would make that face and say "Disgusting!"

That's the way Daddy was looking at me now. Quick as a snake, his hand left my shoulder and worked its way into my hair until it was tangled around his fist. He yanked, making pain shoot through my scalp as he started marching back toward home. No! I needed to get my treasures!

My hands automatically flew up to grab the one wrapped in my hair, small fingers pulling uselessly at his wrist. He was moving fast, though, and I had to run to try to keep up to ease the burning pain in my scalp. My breath came in short gasps of air.

"You come to me when I call you," Daddy ground out in an angry voice. When I glanced up, I could see the muscles were tight in his face.

I must have been supposed to say something because he yanked on my hair again and demanded, "Do you understand me?"

"Y-y-yes, Daddy!" I was quick to answer.

"Don't call me that!" he said, tightening his grip and moving even faster. *Ouchie!!* The sticks and branches on the ground were stabbing into my feet, too. It hurt, but I couldn't cry. If I did, it would be worse. One day. One day, I was gonna be big. And strong. And then...and *then* Daddy and Mama wouldn't be able to hurt me anymore.

In no time at all, we were back at home and Daddy was stomping up the steps, dragging me into the trailer.

"Found her," he announced, shoving me into the living room and letting the screen door slam shut behind us. The force of his push had me falling to the floor, my knees landing hard on the thin, dirty carpet.

I looked up only to feel a sting flash across my cheek along with the sound of a sharp *smack!* My hand flew up to cover the throbbing burn before I'd even realized I'd been hit. Tears stung my eyes. One day, I won't cry if somebody hits me.

"You. Come," Mama said in her super mad voice, "When. We. Call. You!"

She wanted an answer. I knew she did. But my throat was tight from the need to cry, so I bobbed my head up and down. That was the only thing I could do.

"What is the meaning of this?" That was a new voice. I'd never heard that voice before. It sounded different. Fancy.

"You wanted payment," Mama said. "We can't afford what you're askin'. This is all we got."

I peeked up through the dirty curtain of my hair, trying not to let them know that I was looking. I wanted to see what the fancy man looked like but I didn't want Mama to hit me again.

"Explain," the man demanded. Standing in the center of the room, he looked young. Younger than Daddy at least. And he had a black suit on with a tie! How neat was that? I'd never seen anybody wear a tie in real life but it sure made this guy look important. *Fancy*, I thought again.

"What is there to explain?" Daddy asked him. "We need to get out of this hellhole. Look, Mr. Bennett, DeMarco said Mr-" The man made a *tut tut* noise, making Daddy clear his throat before he spoke again. "DeMarco said *your boss* could move us up and out of this piece of shit."

Mr. Bennett tilted his head. "My boss is capable of a great many things."

"DeMarco also said," Mama jumped in, "that your boss isn't picky when it comes to payment."

"That is so," Mr. Bennett casually slid his hand in his pants pockets, "however, you can't expect to get something for nothing."

Slowly, I crawled over to the wall and scooted mostly behind the couch. It never went well for me to get caught in between the grown-ups.

"It's *not* nothing." Mama's voice was getting angry again. I pressed myself up against the wall, pulled my knees to my chest and wrapped my arms around them, making myself as small as I could. If they couldn't see me, they wouldn't hurt me. "It's a freaking kid! I was told a kid might be accepted as payment!"

Ohhh, Mama was mad. Her voice had gotten really high when she finished talking.

"That's correct," Mr. Bennett told her in his very fancy voice, "My employer might be willing to accept a child as payment in order for him to begin a new...project. However, that only applies *if* the child is healthy-"

"She is," Daddy tried to say, but Mr. Bennett just laughed in a mean way. Kind of like the kids I'd seen earlier had laughed at me.

"Healthy? Just look at her," he laughed. Mama and Daddy looked around the room before they seemed to see that Mr. Bennett was pointing right at me. This guy was a good finder. I hoped he didn't have to find me too much. His mean laugh and eyes scared me. "She's skin and bones. When's the last time she had food? Or a bath? I can't even see what she looks like under all the mud. You call that *healthy*? She looks like she's only what...three? Four years old? Does she even have any resilience? Any will to survive? Any fight??"

"She's six," Mama snapped, giving me her mad look. It's not my fault I'm six! I didn't do it on purpose!

Mr. Bennett looked surprised for the first time. His mouth opened as he looked at me, but then it snapped shut. "There is no way that child is six years old unless she's severely malnourished. I can tell you right now, the probability of this child being accepted as payment is very low. The children that *are* accepted need to be well enough to be able to physically handle what they're put through. What else do you have?"

"We have the car and, of course, the trailer here..." Daddy trailed off. I didn't know what was going on, really, except that Mr. Bennett wanted Daddy and Mama to give him something. We didn't have much of anything. Would he leave if they gave him enough stuff? What did he want them to give him? Well, I wasn't going to give him my treasures! I crossed my arms over my chest. He was just gonna have to find something else. He couldn't have my treasures.

I scowled at the thought. I still needed to go back and find them, but I'd have to wait until the man left and Mama and Daddy locked me out again.

Mr. Bennett straightened up, pulled his hands from his pockets, and rubbed them down his jacket. "This appears to have been a waste of our time."

"No, wait," Mama said, moving closer to him. "We'll fix her."

Mr. Bennett just raised his eyebrows up.

"Yes," Daddy agreed with a smile when Mama gave him her mean skinny eyes. "We'll feed her some, clean her up, and she'll be good as new!"

Feed me? They were going to give me food? I was excited at just the thought! For a minute, I thought maybe it might be good that this Mr. Bennett came by. But then, he looked at me for a long time, and seemed to be thinking. I didn't like the way he was looking at me.

"She don't have any school records." Mama sounded like she

was trying to use his fancy tone, but it didn't work very well with her. "She's not in any system at all since she's been home-schooled."

Another long stare from the fancy man. "Is she deaf? Dumb? Does she have brain damage? Does she *speak*?"

I was not *dumb*. Why would he ask that? I could read all by myself! Well...not the big words, but I could read a lot of words, and I learned it all by myself! The fancy man was such a...a...*lazy* for thinking I was dumb. *Ha! You lazy,* I thought.

"Only when we let her." Daddy seemed happy at that idea that I only spoke when they let me. *Ha! Another stupid lazy!* I talked all the time when they weren't there. Most times, I listened outside other peoples houses and copied what they said. I was a really good speaker!

"All right," he finally told them, "I'll present the idea to my employer and I'll let you know the verdict. In the meantime, I suggest, since she seems to be the only thing you have of any value, that you fix her up a bit."

I guess he must have been done talking to them, because he wiggled his tie and walked right out of the house. He didn't seem scared that Mama or Daddy would hit him. I didn't think it would work if I tried that but with the way they looked at me after Mr. Bennett was gone, it made me want to try!

❧ 3 ❧

I didn't even have time to blink when Mama lunged at me. I jerked back, trying to get away but I was just a little too slow. Mama's fingers wrapped around my arm, her fingernails cutting into my skin. I bit hard on my lip to keep myself from making any noises. Mama was already mad. I didn't want to make it worse.

I pulled back, but she acted like I wasn't doing anything at all! Like I was just a dolly. And I felt like one, too! My head jerked back as she yanked me to my feet and pulled me in close to her. "Ugh! You stink!"

Well, I guessed I didn't smell too great, but I didn't want to get back in that cold water. It made my teeth chatter more than the rain did. Daddy stepped close, like he was gonna say something, but then his nose wrinkled up. I was pretty sure my smell didn't change since he found me in the woods. I almost wanted to sniff myself just to see.

Mama pulled me to the door and pushed me outside, back into the cold rain. I stumbled on unsteady legs before I took my chance to escape and rushed down the porch steps. "We'll deal with her tomorrow. There's no point in cleaning her up if they aren't gonna take the deal. Besides, maybe the rain'll wash off some of that dirt."

I didn't wait around to hear any more. I ran as fast as my legs could carry me, right past the big, shiny, rumbling car that I hadn't noticed earlier. My body ached from all the bruises, my hair and clothes were plastered to my skin, and I was so hungry I bet I could've eaten that whole pizza that boy had talked about earlier. Still, I ran, looking back once to make sure they weren't going to follow me.

I was going to get my treasures. I had to hide them so Mama wouldn't try to give them to the fancy man. My feet splashed through puddles, my toes squishing in the cool mud, but I didn't care. Slipping and sliding, I made my way back to the front of the trailers by the road, watching the ground for my treasures. It was getting dark and I was moving so fast I almost missed my dolly!

She was lying where I'd left her in the dirt, only it wasn't dirt anymore it was mud. The rain that came down almost tried to wash her away into a puddle. I scooped her up quick and looked for Baby Bear, but I couldn't find him. Spinning in circles didn't help, so I fell to my knees and shoved my hands frantically through the mud, pushing it away in case it hid Baby Bear.

But he wasn't there! He wasn't anywhere! Sobs started in my chest, making my shoulders shake. "I'm sorry, Baby Bear," I whispered. I shouldn't have left him. A dog might have got him, or somebody might have thrown him away. Tears trembled on my lashes.

A splashing noise came from behind me and I spun around, thinking Mama or Daddy had come to get me. It wasn't them, though. It was just the fancy man. What was he doing here? Didn't he go home?

The fancy man stood there in the rain holding a black umbrella in one hand and sliding a cell phone into his pocket with his other. His head was tilted and he was looking at me funny again. I'd watched TV through one of the neighbor's windows. There were big monkeys on there that looked the way he was looking at me just then. Did he think he was a monkey? Maybe there was some damage in *his* brain.

He was lucky he was a little ways away from me still and I was looking for Baby Bear or I'd have run away already.

"Hello," he called quietly.

Was he talking to me? I looked behind me, but I didn't see anybody else. I really hoped he wasn't talking to me. I was too busy for the fancy man, because I needed to find Baby Bear!

I looked back to the fancy man and he squatted down close to the ground. "What's your name?"

Even squatting down, he was taller than me. I didn't like that, so I stood up. That would make it easier to run anyway.

"Cat got your tongue?"

"I'm not sposed to talk to strangers," I whispered, shuffling my feet around, and squeezing my fingers tight around my dolly. My tummy got the flutters again. Most grownups didn't talk to me.

The fancy man smiled. Not a big smile. The kind where a person thinks something's just a little funny but not a whole lot funny.

"Did your parents teach you that?" His voice was quiet when he asked me that. I don't know if he didn't want the neighbors to hear or if he thought I'd run away if he was too loud.

I didn't say anything, just wiggled my bare toes in the mud and made sure to keep my eyes on him in case he decided to try to hit me. After what felt like a long time, he sighed.

"You know...once two people are introduced, they aren't strangers anymore. Maybe if we introduce ourselves – "

My head snapped up right then. "No!"

The fancy man looked really surprised, but I couldn't let him think that he was saying the right thing. If he really did have damage in his brain, he could get kidnapped if he didn't know the truth!

"Just cuz you know somebody's name don't mean they're not a stranger," I told him in my best schoolteacher voice. "You still are sposed to be careful."

The fancy man made a small, laugh.

"You're right. You're absolutely right. Did your parents teach you that?" I was still watching him but he didn't move. He stayed right where he was, and that helped make some of the flutters go away.

"No. They don't teach me anything. You have to be very careful or you can get kidnapped and if the police don't find the bad guys fast, you can be gone for-eh-verr." I drew out the sound of that last word because I wanted to make sure he knew that word meant a long time.

He shuffled a little closer, but I was too smart for that and took two quick, giant steps back. My daddy had tried that trick before. He didn't move closer to me. That was good. I didn't like it when people got too close or tried to touch me.

"Your parents didn't teach you that? Then where'd you learn it?" I was surprised that he sounded like he really wanted to know. Maybe I should tell him. That way he could learn too and fix some of the damage in his brain.

"I learned all about stranger danger from the TV. There's a show on there called The First Forty-Eight. It's a very 'portant show and you can learn about bad guys on there."

He looked confused for a minute. "I didn't see a TV in your house..."

Well, of course he didn't. The only TV was in Mama and Daddy's room. I did a big sigh like I'd seen some of the grownup neighbors do.

"That's cuz there's not one in there. Well, 'cept for Daddy's TV in his room but I'm not allowed in there." I wouldn't want to go in there either!

"If you don't have a TV, how do you watch your show?" His damage must be getting worse because he looked even more confused then. I guessed I should probably tell him about this part too in case he didn't have a TV either. He should know how to find one.

I looked, real quick, at the closest neighbor's house. It was a quick look because I didn't want him to jump at me when I wasn't looking. Nope. He was still there in the same spot.

I crouched down and waved at him to do the same thing. "Look over there," I whispered, when he did, pointing at the neighbor's window. When people were sharing secrets, they were supposed to whisper. I saw some of the other kids do that and it made me feel proud to share a secret for once.

The fancy man turned so he was looking where I pointed. When he got just a little bit lower, he could look in through the curtains in the window and see the TV hanging high up on the wall.

My voice stayed at a whisper when I told him, "If you don't have a TV, lots of other people have some. You can watch theirs to learn about stranger danger so you don't get taken away."

When his eyes went from the window back to me, he stared at me really hard for a long time. It made the flutters come back into my belly and I stepped back again when his lips made that funny smile that wasn't an all-the-way-smile.

"That's very smart, Taryn. You're a very smart little girl." Nobody had ever called me smart before and I wasn't sure that I liked it when he did it. There was a look in his eyes when he talked to me then that made me step back even more. I was close to the trees and could hide in them if I needed to.

Even if he hadn't hit me, or called me names, or made me cry, the fancy man was still a stranger. I watched him warily as he rose back to his full height, still staring at me with that weird smile on his face.

He turned away with his umbrella still in one hand and

pulled his cell phone from his pocket with his free hand. I backed up again so that I was just inside the trees. I'd keep looking for Baby Bear when the man left.

"But wait, Taryn," he said suddenly, like he'd just had an idea, and turned back around. I didn't think he was going to hit me since his hands were full but I took another step back just in case he thought about it.

"What if...," he began, "just what *if*...I *wanted* to be taken away?"

What? Why would he want to be taken away?

He took a step toward me and I stepped back again, my bare feet getting poked by sticks.

"What if the place I was at was so bad that I *wanted* to be taken away? Maybe that would be better for me. To be taken away. What do you think about that, Taryn?"

My throat and mouth felt suddenly more dry than it had in a long time. I swallowed as much spit as I could form. Sometimes, I thought about getting taken away to school. Is that what he meant? Or did *he* want to take me away? "I think...if you wanted to get taken away...I think you should watch the Dateline show too so you can see what happens to people that don't get found."

With that, I turned and ran, ducking and dodging the branches that tried to get in my way. I had thought he might come after me, but the only thing that followed was a long, loud sound of laughter echoing through the night.

❧ 4 ☙

After the fancy man had left, I went to watch some TV. I really liked a lot of the shows on there. There was one on there called Jeopardy, and it was one of my favorites! I watched it so much that I had most of the questions memorized. When I got too sleepy, I spent the night hiding underneath the back porch of one of my neighbors. It wasn't as bad as some people might think. It was actually pretty nice and quiet and I had my dolly, so that made me feel better. There were some snakes under there, but they didn't have the pointy heads, and they stayed away from me, so it was okay.

There was also a mommy cat. I guess I got too close to her babies and she scratched me, but I wasn't mad at her. I thought it was pretty nice that she was trying to keep her babies safe. My belly growled and ached all night and I had gotten pretty thirsty, so I was glad it was raining because that meant I had plenty to drink!

The school bus woke me up like it always did. That let me know it was time to go watch some of my learning shows! There were some kids that lived a little ways down the street that really *were* homeschooled. It wasn't like my homeschool that Mama talked about. These kids had computers and got to watch videos showing them how to do stuff. Even though I didn't have paper, I still did the work with them. All I needed was a stick!

My belly grumbled as I walked down the street. It felt sick but there was nothing in there to *make* it sick. One time, when I'd been super hungry, I'd tried eating some leaves like I'd seen the animals do, but that was gross and didn't make my belly feel any better, so I didn't do that anymore.

I was really excited when I got to the house and saw that they'd left the window open. I loved it when they did that because then I could hear the videos better. The kids were much bigger than me, but they were also different ages so that made it more fun. I could see what they were *all* doing, and that was good because sometimes the stuff was too hard. I got there just in time to hear Cassie's 'word of the day'. The words of the day were never any of the words that Mama said to me. Extrapolate. I said that word to myself fifty times. *Knowing what might happen because it already did happen. Extrapolate.*

I realized I extrapolated all the time! Like when I missed the dishes, I *extrapolated* that Mama would get mad and yell at me or hit me. This was such a fun game! I had just finished one of the long multiplication problems when I heard the yelling from the trailer park. A ball of dread wound its way through my already sore belly. It sounded like Daddy, but he was supposed to be at work. Why would he be home already?

That's when I remembered. Last night they'd said something about waiting till tomorrow to deal with me. And it was tomorrow! I panicked. Not even thinking about doing the next problem, I dropped my stick in the dirt and ran back toward the trailer. They'd told me I had to come when they called. I needed to hurry or I was going to be in trouble.

When I got back, Daddy was waiting outside with the water hose. He was wearing his old pants with the holes in them. He didn't wear them too much because he had ones without holes in it that he said were his nice pants. His face was red, and his eyebrows were low and close to his nose. That was his yelling face.

"It's about time! I've been waiting on you for ten minutes!" He pointed at the watch on his wrist, as if I knew anything about that.

I could do lots of things with numbers. I could count really high, write them down with a stick, add them, subtract them, and even multiply and divide them. But, I didn't know how to tell time unless it had the real numbers and not the ones the Romans used. Daddy's watch was a Roman watch and, I didn't have much need to tell time anyway because I didn't usually have anywhere to be.

His face was still red, and he looked like he was waiting for me to say something, so I whispered out a, "Sorry," hoping that would be enough.

Mama came out then. I guess she must have heard Daddy. "What are you doing?" she asked.

I didn't know if she was talking to me, but before I could answer her anyway, Daddy said, "I'm gonna hose her down!"

"You can't do that!" Mama told him. "We've got nosy ass neighbors. Do you want them calling Child Services?"

That was a new term for me. Child services. What could that mean? I knew service was to do something for people. Mrs. Jessup, who lived a few trailers away, was always talking about 'how awful the service was'. Was it a place where kids did services for people? That didn't sound very good. I already did services like the dishes. I didn't want to have to do any more!

"Fine," Daddy said in a snappy tone. "You think you know how to do it? *You* clean her up then!"

Daddy threw the water hose down and stomped back into the house, slamming the door behind him. Mama gave a big sigh, grabbed my arm and followed after him, stomping the whole way. I had to move my legs really fast to keep up with her. I really wished she would stop touching me so much! She always hurt me when she touched me.

Mama yanked open the trailer door and roughly pushed me through. This time I tripped but I didn't fall on the floor, which made me happy. Mama always said that being on the floor was weak, so I thought she'd be happy too, but she just looked even more mad. Did she *want* me to fall down?

She grabbed me again, really tight, and pulled me down the little hallway and into the bathroom. Oh, no! Was she going to make me shower again already? I shivered just thinking about it. Maybe I could make it super quick. That wouldn't be so bad.

Mama must have had a different idea, though, because she turned the shower on, but she didn't leave like she usually did. She held the bottom of my shirt between two fingers and made the disgusted face, then she just started yanking all my clothes off, throwing my dolly across the room when she got in the way of my shirt coming off. Mama had done this before one time when we lived at our old apartment and one of the neighbors had given me a pretty new dress. That had made Mama *really* mad.

"Go find her some clothes," she yelled to Daddy.

I didn't know what was going on here, but it could not be good, so I did the absolute worst thing possible. I tried to run away. I pulled my arm away from Mama, trying to get away from her. She grabbed hold of my arm, holding it so tightly I thought it was going to snap in half! It hurt so much that, even knowing how much Mama didn't like it when I cried, the tears came anyway.

Her hand swung up. I barely saw it move before I felt the burn on the side of my face. It didn't matter how much I fought; Mama still got her way. She *always* got her way. One day, I'd be strong. So strong Mama wouldn't get her way anymore. Then, I would get *my* way! I really hoped she hadn't hurt my dolly.

Before I even knew she was going to do it, she shoved my

whole body under the icy cold water. Her hand tangled in the back of my hair, holding my head under the spray. In seconds, I was drenched and shivering. The water was making it hard to breathe. I tried to pull my head away, but she wouldn't let go. Long seconds went by as I struggled and kicked, trying to move my head and get some air. All I did was slip around the tub.

Just when I thought she was finally going to kill me, a hard, strong hand yanked me back out of the spray. I gasped in air, coughing and choking.

"...kill her then we won't get shit!" Daddy was yelling at Mama. They both looked really angry.

He threw some clothes on the floor of the bathroom and stomped back out and Mama gave me a look I knew very well. It was the one she gave me right before she hurt me usually. She smiled, opened a bottle and poured something over my head. I didn't know what it was. I'd never seen it before, but it smelled really nice. Mama doesn't smile a lot, but I want her to keep doing it, so I smiled back at her.

Mama dug her hands into my hair, spreading the stuff around then shoved my head back under the spray. Immediately, I knew it had been a trick. Bubbles poured into my eyes, burning them. I shrieked, trying to wipe it off, but it wouldn't go away. My eyes just kept burning and burning, while I cried. And Mama laughed. I couldn't see her, but I could hear her.

I tipped my head back, trying to get the water to make the pain go away. For the first time ever, I was glad to be in the cold shower because it was helping the burn in my eyes.

Then I felt more thick liquid being dumped on me. It started at the top of my shoulder and oozed slowly down my back. I braced myself because I knew the game then. This was another hurting game. Sure enough, within seconds, a hard brush was pressed against my skin, scrubbing to get the dirt off. I flinched, biting my lip to keep from making any more noise, though the sobs escaped anyway.

Thankfully, Mama wouldn't be able to tell I was crying aside from the noise because of the water. When I could finally blink my eyes open again, there was a bad ache and burn in them. I could see Mama was smiling while she scrubbed me with a brush. It made me sad to think that she'd be happy that I was hurting.

She brought the brush to my arm, scrubbing away. That hurt pretty bad too and it left long, red lines on my skin each time she moved it. It was the same brush she made me use when I had to scrub the floors. More tears mixed with the cold water rolling down my face. I tried to think of something else. Maybe if I stayed quiet, she would finish faster and I could go hide in the woods again.

I looked away from her, my free hand coming up to scrub at my still burning eyes. It was blue. Vaguely, I wondered why that happened. Was the bubbly stuff turning me a different color? It smelled good, but I didn't think I wanted to turn blue. That wasn't even my favorite color!

In the next second, I decided it didn't really matter enough to tell Mama to stop. She jerked me around, making my hip bang on the faucet, causing a sharp cry to tear from my throat. I didn't want to make her any more angry than she already was.

"Shut up!" she snapped.

I wanted to tell her I hadn't meant to do it, but I didn't think she would care and would probably hurt me some more for saying that, so I just stayed as quiet as I could and let her jerk me around. I looked to the bottom of the bathtub, moving wherever she put me. The water started off a grayish-black color, but as I watched, red started to swirl in it as it ran toward the hole in the bottom of the tub.

I was too weak to fight her, and I didn't want her to hold my head under the water again. It was so scary not being able to breathe. There was nothing I could do except stand there, shivering, shaking, teeth clacking like crazy, and sobbing as she did what she wanted. She scrubbed and scrubbed my head and my body until the water ran a pinkish-red color, then she snatched me out of the tub, uncaring that I slipped a lot, banging my knees and elbows on the tub.

The water turned off and a long t-shirt was suddenly pulled over my head, feeling like it was swallowing me whole. It was so long it went down past my feet. Mama grabbed my arm and started yanking me back down the hallway to the living room. I couldn't make my teeth stop chattering. It reminded me of the winters when I had to sleep under porches. That was the warmest spot because the warm would go through the floors of people's houses and I wouldn't be as cold.

I tripped over the shirt, but Mama was quick to yank me up, so I was dangling in the air by my arm. It felt like she was going to pull my arm off! A whimper escaped me because it hurt where she was holding me, and it hurt at my shoulder. I knew Mama wouldn't care, though. She'd just tell me to shut up again, but it was hard to do that sometimes. The sounds just came out!

The light gray shirt stuck to my body. Mama carried me into the living room and dropped me on the floor. I turned my head away, looking at the floor as I tried to hide the tears that still streamed down my face. I hoped they would think it was the shivers that made my body shake. I thought they probably were, but the sobs trying to get out of my chest sure didn't help any.

The *whir* of a fan came on, blowing on me and making my soaked hair fly all over. Daddy pulled a chair up close and started pulling and tugging at my hair. I flinched when it felt like he was ripping my hair out. My hands automatically flew up to my head, trying to protect it from whatever he was doing to it.

A firm *smack* and pain burst through my hand. I snatched it back quick, more tears rolling down my face. I cradled my hand to my chest, just letting him do it. A big red mark was on my hand and it looked like it was getting bigger just from watching it! I looked away fast because I didn't want it to get any bigger.

"Awww. Are you crying like a wittle baaaaabyyyy?" Mama asked, getting down on the floor with me.

I shook my head as much as I could with Daddy pulling my hair, trying not to think about how much so many parts of me were hurting.

"I-i-it's w-w-w-water," I told her through my chattering teeth, hoping she wouldn't notice the way my voice shook, or at least just think it was because of the cold.

"It's just w-w-w-waaaater?" she asked me in a mean voice. I nodded my head anyway, wincing at the yank of my hair. "I think you're l-l-l-lyyyyyying."

Frantically, I shook my head, my fear making me not care as much about the pulling and tugging on my hair.

"And you know what happens to little kids that lie, don't you?"

I nodded, because I knew what happened, but then I quickly shook my head because I didn't *want* it to happen! Mama was already nodding as she went into the kitchen. I wanted to run away but with Daddy doing something to my hair, all I could do was sit there, shiver, and wait for her to come back.

❧ 5 ❧

Small whimpers slipped from my throat as I watched Mama in the kitchen. I knew what was coming but that didn't make it any easier. Though this wasn't the first time she'd done this, every time I hoped it'd be the last. Daddy gave a particularly hard yank on my hair, making my head jerk back. I couldn't pull my eyes away from Mama, though.

She reached under the cabinet and pulled out one of the really old glass dishes under there. A bowl this time. Then she grabbed several more things and came back over to me. The whimpers and tears kept coming. I couldn't stop them. Most of the time, that made Mama mad, but this time she looked really happy.

"Do you remember what this is, Taryn?" Mama waved the glass bowl in front of my face. It felt like there was a big, hot ball in my throat, so I couldn't say anything. Still, I bobbed my head up and down.

"This," she said, like she didn't care that I knew and just wanted to keep talking, "was one of my mom's antique dishes." She tilted it from side to side, letting the light sparkle through it. If I didn't know what it was for, I might would have thought it was pretty. "And before she died, she told me she really, *really* wanted you to have it."

My breath started coming in big gasps as I felt Daddy's hands come to my shoulders, holding me still. My body just tried to jerk away. I didn't do it on purpose. My body just wanted to run, but he was too strong.

"So, I'm gonna let you have it, Taryn. Just like your grandma wanted." I didn't want it! I shook my head really fast, but she didn't slow down at all. With a big swing, the hand holding the glass bowl flew through the air. I flinched, my whole body jerking and trying to be ready.

The bowl landed right on the side of my head with a big *thump!* It felt like my brain shook around inside my head. My whole head hurt, especially on the inside, and I was really dizzy. I felt like I'd spun in a bunch of circles. If Daddy hadn't been holding onto me, I would've fallen over.

My eyes opened up, but everything was blurry and there was wetness on the side of my face. I reached up to wipe it away and my hand came back red. It was a shiny red. There was glass all over my lap and on the floor.

There was a loud noise that was giving me a headache. Daddy let go of my shoulders and started back with his tugging and pulling.

Mama was suddenly right in my face, pointing her finger at me. "Shut up!" I snapped my mouth closed and the noise cut off. I hadn't known I'd been screaming. Everything hurt so much! I was having a hard time thinking straight and I really, all of the sudden, just wanted to take a nap.

My breaths were still coming fast when Mama made me stand up. All of the glass fell down to the floor. Mama used a broom to put them all in a pile, then made me stand on the pile. I knew I had to be really still and try not to move because that would make it hurt even more. It was hard to do because I was trembling a whole lot! I couldn't stop crying. I was so scared and hurt so much. My nose started to get drippy.

Then Mama held up a little brush in one hand and the soap for dishes in the other. I watched her pour the soap onto the little brush. I hated this part too, but I was too little to fight! I wanted to fight. I wanted to kick her really hard until she left me alone, but I was on the glass and it was already cutting my feet. Any time I tried to move them, Daddy would give me a little push, making the glass cut me even more.

So, when Mama pinched my nose shut and shoved the little brush in my mouth, there was nothing I could do except cry, choke, and try not to throw up. Bubbles filled my mouth and the soap taste made me feel sick. I had seen some of the families in the neighborhood doing something called 'praying'. They thought really hard about something good happening and it did. I had tried it before, but it never worked for me. Right then, with my mouth full of soap, my feet cut up from glass, bruises covering me, and blood dripping from my hair, I thought they were stupid.

I thought those prayer people were just making stuff up because it *never* worked for me. Not once. But I wished it would.

Sickness rolled up my belly in a big wave and I gagged. My stomach churned, but there was nothing in there to come up and Mama just laughed when she saw that. When she and Daddy finished, they pushed me into the corner of the room.

"Don't move from that spot until you're dry!" Daddy told me in his angry tone. He was holding a brush that had so much strands of hair on it that I couldn't even see what kind of brush it was except that it had a short handle.

I wasn't going to move anyway! As long as they left me alone, I would stay right there in that spot. It was cold, but at least I didn't have to walk on my cut feet! What a stupid lazy he was to think I'd want to walk around when it hurt. Is that what *he* did? I couldn't picture him ever being hurt. Maybe it was because he was so mean. Maybe if I were mean I wouldn't be hurt either!

I didn't know if I could be mean, though. I didn't do a very good job at that with my dolly and Baby Bear. I let out a sigh, scooted back against the wall and leaned the not hurt side of my head up against the wall. My body felt really yuck. I knew I shouldn't take a nap. Daddy liked to scare me when I was sleeping. He might wake me up by throwing one of his brown bottles at me.

I wished I could go outside and hide under the porch. I didn't think Mama and Daddy could fit under there. I pulled my knees up to my chest and wrapped my arms around them as I sat there. The shirt was still all the way down to the floor. It even covered my feet up.

Red was coming up through the shirt from my knees. I knew it was blood. I was smart enough to know what that was and what it did. I also knew that most people have around a gallon of blood in their body. I didn't know what a gallon felt like, but I hoped all of mine wasn't leaking out! It sure *looked* like a lot. It was all in the tub, all over my face, and now the shirt was taking a bunch of it!

I wondered if there was a way to get it out of the shirt and back inside me. My face scrunched up as I thought about that. Maybe there was a TV show about that. I'd have to look through a lot of windows to find one. I liked to find out about new stuff. One of the kids in another trailer called it *learning*. I definitely learned something from Mama. Crying only makes things worse. That idea made me think about my treasures. I couldn't stop worrying about my Dolly and hoping she was okay after Mama had thrown her into the wall.

After a long, *long* while of Mama and Daddy talking about their 'new house', it got a lot quieter. They left me where I was, sitting on the floor in front of the fan, to go to their bedroom. Probably to watch their TV. It must be nice to just be able to watch whatever you want all the time. One day I will have my own TV and then I can watch the discover station all by myself whenever I want!

Mama and Daddy wouldn't come out for a long time. I extrapolate that because they usually stay in there. Plus, how would they know if I got up before I was all dried? I didn't think they would, and *most* parts were dry, I thought. So, I got up, being extra careful of my feet that had blood still on them and tried to be as sneaky as Daddy usually was when I tiptoed down the hallway. I had to keep a good watch on their bedroom door because I didn't want them to catch me. Super quick, I went into the bathroom and snatched up my dolly. I'd look her over when it was safe.

I peeked out first to make sure their door was still closed. It was, so I sneaked my way back down the hallway and to the front door, which I opened, and went outside. I felt much better being out there. Not my ouchies, though. They still hurt a lot. And so did my belly. It didn't grumble anymore. It just hurt. Still on my tippy toes, I held up the end of the shirt with one hand and went super fast into the trees.

The whole way, I kept trying to spit out the taste of the bubbles in my mouth. I hated it when she did that and I really, really wished people would stop touching me. Every time somebody touched me, it hurt. I was so tired of hurting. Why couldn't they just leave me alone?

I found my secret spot and started looking over my dolly. I had already lost Baby Bear. If my dolly was broken, I didn't know what I would do. Sometimes, when I went into the woods, I would pretend that I lived in one of the other houses. That I had a mommy and daddy that didn't hurt me all the time. I wanted to be somebody...*anybody*...different.

After a little while of my tummy hurting and making sure my dolly was okay, I heard the school bus come again. Most times, I was excited to see the bus and the other kids because seeing them be happy made me happy. That day, I wasn't. I was mad!

How come those kids got to be happy and not me? How come *they* got to eat pizza and watch TV and go to a real school?

The tears tried to come again, but I pressed my lips together real tight and made them go away. *No!* No more tears! No more crying! No more being a baby or a...a...a *stupid lazy*! I sniffled, wiping my drippy nose on the shirt sleeve.

Soon, squeals of laughter echoed all around me. Ugh! Why were they being so loud anyway?! I plopped my dolly on the knee of my bloody shirt.

"We don't care do we?"

"Nooo," I had my dolly say in a high, lady voice. "We don't care about those stupid lazies!" I crossed my arms over my chest but had to be quick to grab my dolly when she almost fell off my lap. There was more laughing. I looked at my dolly and rolled my eyes like I'd seen one of the kids do yesterday.

"Fine!" I said in a huff. My dolly really looked like she wanted to go see what they were all so happy about. "Let's go see, then!" Sometimes, my dolly could be so irritating!

Scooping her up, I carried her over to the same edge of the woods we'd been at yesterday. This time, I was scared to go out to the other kids. They had made my tummy hurt and I had felt like I was...yucky. Well, my tummy already hurt and I didn't want to feel yucky again, so I just wasn't going to go out there!

I peeked around the edge of a big tree, trying to see what all the kids were doing. They were all crowded around something. I stood on my tippy toes, but I *still* couldn't see what it was. I looked at the tree beside me, trying to figure out if I could climb it so I could see. I didn't think I could. It was pretty big. Plus, I had my dolly. I didn't want to lose her, too if I put her down. I would have to get closer.

I went back down the side of the trees a little ways, then ran out quick to get behind the closest trailer. My heart was beating really fast. I peeked around the corner of the trailer, making sure nobody had seen me. The coast was clear, so I ran to the next one. My feet started hurting then, because I had been being fast instead of careful and had stepped on some rocks and sticks.

"This was not a good idea," I whispered to my dolly. She just stared at me, like she didn't know what I was talking about. She couldn't fool me!

I peeked around the new corner and was close enough to see but there were so many kids! I had to get a little bit closer. Hmmm...I looked at the ground. I could go under the trailer. I did that all the time. There were holes under there that were big enough for me to get through...but...I probably would get dirty.

Mama's face flashed through my mind as she held me under the water and laughed. I shook with fear and had to squeeze my lips tight together to keep the whimpers from coming out. No. I wouldn't go under the trailer. I didn't want that to happen again, so I would just have to wait.

After what felt like for-eh-verrrr, the kids started losing interest and moving away. Finally! When a little gap opened up, I moved around just enough to see the boy from yesterday. The one who was getting pizza at his house and told me I was like trash. He was sitting on the steps to his trailer and...he was holding a baby!!

I had seen those before. Not up close, but I knew what they were, and I felt bad for it. A baby meant less food. Somebody was going to be hungry − probably the baby. It couldn't get its own food.

Even though I had never been around them, I was pretty sure I didn't like babies. From what I had seen, they were loud and messy.

The boy was holding the baby really carefully and being very still. His head was bent close to the baby's face. Without any warning, the baby suddenly opened its mouth and white stuff flew out of there. It came out really fast and got all over the boy's face. I felt my face twist up. I was pretty sure that was the disgust face. Though...I had to admit, it was pretty funny that it had thrown up in that boy's face. Maybe that baby wasn't too bad.

He did *not* like that at all. He yelled, the baby started crying, and all the kids screamed and ran away. The baby's face turned red as it screamed and screamed. I covered my ears up. Yep. I was for sure then. I did *not* like babies.

A lady came over and, for a minute, I was really worried she was going to hit the baby and tell it to shut up like Mama did. I took a step. I didn't like babies, but that baby didn't know to be quiet. My mouth opened up. I didn't know what I was going to say, but I didn't have to be worried.

The lady picked up the baby, super careful, and wiped it with a towel while talking in a really quiet voice. Then she wiped the boy's face and they all went inside. What had just happened? She didn't hit the baby or the boy. Maybe she was waiting till she got inside. That made sense. She probably didn't want people to call the child services either.

I was curious enough to go peek inside the window, but a hand touched my shoulder before I could do it. I flinched, wondering if Mama or Daddy had found me, and I jerked away and turned around. I didn't like to be touched!

It was the girl from yesterday. The one with the pretty ribbons. She looked at me, as if she wasn't sure about something. I backed up, because I remembered the bad feeling from yesterday.

"Are you...," she stopped for a minute, biting her lip, and I tilted my head just a little bit while I waited for her to spit it out. "Are you the girl from yesterday?"

Why would she ask me that? How many people that were 'gross' and 'yucky' like me did she know? Should I tell her I was the same girl? If I did, would she get her friends and make me sad again? I didn't know what to do or say.

"Your hair is really pretty," she said. I blinked. Was that a trick? Nobody had ever told me my hair was pretty. Slowly, I reached up and lifted some to look at it. When my hand touched it, I thought I had grabbed something else...like a feather. It was so soft! I pulled it around to look at it. It wasn't wet anymore. It was long and...white. I thought only old people had white hair.

I looked from it back to the girl, still not saying anything. What was the right thing to say? Her friends had been mean to me yesterday. I guessed *she* hadn't, but did that make it okay?

"You're bleeding. Are you okay?"

Was I okay? What did that even mean? She had a weird look to her face that I wasn't sure I'd ever really seen up close. Her eyebrows were pulled down and her eyes were moving back and forth from mine to the side of my head that Mama had hit. I wasn't sure how, exactly, but I felt like this was important.

Was I okay? Well...I supposed in that moment, I wasn't being touched or bothered too much, so I bobbed my head up and down, trying to ignore the sharp pain that went through it when I moved.

The girl didn't look like she believed me. Why would she even ask me that if she was just going to think I was lying anyway? She didn't make much sense.

"Well...," she said, moving from one foot to the other. "My name's Katie and...I just wanted to give this back to you." She held her hand out and I jumped back quick before she could touch me.

Only, she wasn't trying to touch me. She was giving me...Baby Bear? I reached forward, snatching it from her hand and pulling him to my chest in a tight hug. I thought he was gone forever!! I thought...why did she have Baby Bear? I looked from him to her.

"I found him in the dirt so I took him home and asked my mom to fix him. She gave him a bath...," she paused at my gasp of horror. Had she put Baby Bear's head under the water?? "And she sewed him up for you. He should be good as new..." she moved from foot to foot again.

I was distracted for a minute by her weird dance. Then, I focused on Baby Bear, looking him over to make sure he was okay. He wasn't dirty anymore and I couldn't even see where the stuffing had been coming out of him. Was her mom a doctor? What was I supposed to do now?

Should I just go home? Or was I supposed to shake her hand? I had seen people do that before. Ugh! I really didn't want her to touch me. What else did people do? Oh!! I knew!

Raising my hand up near my head, I moved it back and forth, *waving* at her. People did that all the time. The girl looked confused for a minute, then she said, "Okay...see you later!" She turned around and ran away.

I frowned, my hand falling down to my side. Had I done something wrong? Was it not the right thing? Then, the girl ran up the steps to a trailer, turned around, and did the best thing ever. She smiled and waved at me.

Yes!! I felt a lot better seeing that, so I pulled my lips up and apart a little bit so my teeth showed and waved at her again before I squeezed my treasures tight and ran back into the woods before her friends could see me.

6

I really didn't want to go back home, but Mama and Daddy were being different than normal, so I thought it *might… maybe…*okay, it probably would be a good idea. It felt like worms were crawling around in my belly as I tippy toed back through the woods to my house. It sure took a lot of work to tippy toe. I wasn't exactly sure why I did it except that I had seen the other kids do it when they were trying to be sneaky and didn't want people to hear them.

Well, I for sure didn't want Mama and Daddy to hear me, so that must be the right thing to do.

There was a shiny car parked in the grass by Mama's trailer. Was it the fancy man? I thought it was. He's the only person I could ever remember that came to visit that might have a shiny car. Oh, no! If he was here, Mama and Daddy would be out of their room and know I wasn't sitting in the corner!

I was really scared about what they would do if they knew I had gotten up. I chewed on my lip while I tried to figure out if I should just go in or find somewhere to hide. I stood frozen, knowing no matter which one I did, I was going to get in trouble when I heard a door open.

I looked up quick to see if Mama had come outside, but the door was still closed, so I turned, searching for where the sound had come from. It was the fancy man! He was dressed in another suit with a tie but the best thing was that he hadn't gone inside yet! He was messing with something on his tie. Maybe if I just tippy toed inside, they would still be in their room. I headed up the steps.

"Hey, there," the fancy man called out. I looked over, but he was looking at me so I stopped even though I didn't want to. Why did he want to talk to me *again?* Weren't grown-ups supposed to talk to other grown-ups? His eyes looked over me, from my bare toes up to my head where his eyes stopped on the bloody side. Then he looked from me to the house like he was trying to figure out a problem. "Do you live here?"

I tilted my head, trying to figure out what was going on here. I met the fancy man yesterday. Right there in that house. Then he talked to me by the woods. Why was he asking if I lived there now? Was it the damage in his brain? I nodded, really big and slow, so he could take his time to make sure he knew I was making the 'yes' motion.

"I thought they only had one kid," he said, but not like he was talking to me. I felt my eyebrows crinkle as I looked around to see if somebody else was around. There wasn't. Just me. Either he was talking to me super quiet, or he was talking to somebody I couldn't see. So, taking a guess, I very slowly nodded again.

He looked surprised then and his mouth dropped open. "Taryn?" he asked.

Who else would I be? He must be having a hard time remembering stuff. I nodded again, real slow because of his damage. I looked back at the door, ready to go before Mama and Daddy caught me outside.

"Wow. What a difference a good cleaning makes!"

Well, I wouldn't call it a *good* cleaning. There hadn't been anything good about it! I felt my face twist again. I wasn't sure what face I made, but it made him laugh. For some reason, my body jerked back real quick when he did that. I looked at the door again, trying to see if I could see Mama or Daddy moving around in there on the other side of the screen door.

"Your mom and dad home?" I nodded again. Did that mean it was okay for me to go inside then? Did he want to go inside? Was it okay for me to let him inside? I wasn't sure. I thought people were supposed to knock before they went inside somebody's house that wasn't their own.

The fancy man didn't say anything else, so I guessed it must be okay to leave. Keeping my treasures close, I turned and went up the steps, reaching for the door handle. Suddenly, the door was shoved open from the other side, slamming into my face.

I fell backwards, tripping over the long shirt I was wearing. I felt my body falling and I moved my foot, feeling for the porch. There was nothing but empty air. I was too close to the steps!

I knew I was going to fall and it was going to hurt my already hurting body. My eyes opened wide, looking helplessly at Mama. I don't know why some part of me still hoped she'd help me. Mama never helped me. She just smiled, but then her eyes moved past me, over my shoulder.

I felt hands on my back, catching me, lifting me up, and placing me back on my feet. I couldn't think past the feeling of hands on me. Immediately, I was jumping away, placing myself sideways between Mama and the fancy man and moving away from them both. I didn't want them to sneak up on me, so I stayed where I could see them, my eyes bouncing back and forth. My back felt like there were things crawling on it where the man had touched me. I didn't like it.

"Didn't I tell you to stay there?" Mama snapped.

She reached for me, her hand making the grabby motion, but my skin still had the crawlies from the last touch, so I ducked out of the way without even thinking about it. She hated it when

I did that. Her face turned red and it looked like she was going to yell.

I started to nod my head, but the fancy man started talking instead. "It was my fault. I asked her outside so I could see what she looked like without all the dirt."

Mama looked from him to me. My eyes were big in my face because the man had just lied to Mama! Either that or his brain had a lot more damage than I thought! I couldn't believe it! I don't think Mama believed him either because she still gave me a mean look.

His hand lifted toward me and I jerked back quick. Was he going to hit me? Even if he wasn't, I didn't want him touching me.

"What's that?" he asked, pointing at the side of my head.

Mama gave him a really nasty look. "It's blood. What the hell do you think it is?"

The fancy man's eyes did a neat trick then. They went up and around in a circle! I decided I was going to try that too! Though, I might not be able to because it could be from his brain. Maybe he didn't do it on purpose.

"I see that. What I want to know is why? Do you think the child will be as valuable if she's got a concussion? He accepts children as payment, though, as I'm sure you're aware, damaged goods don't have nearly as much value."

Wow! There were some new words in there! A...conk shun? I didn't know what that was yet, but I would have to see if I could find out! What did damaged goods mean? I had heard about goods and services. That's why I didn't want to be a child service. Was he trying to say I was a child good? That didn't make any sense. Buuut...child service didn't make much sense either. Maybe he was thinking of the other 'good'. If so, I could tell him right then that Mama would *not* agree that I was a good child.

"*You* said he probably wouldn't want her anyway!" Mama told him.

"No. What I said was that I'd present the idea to my employer and in the meantime, you should make her a bit more...appealing on the chance that he *is* interested. I see you've at least partially done that...or...made an attempt at any rate. At least she's clean. Has she been fed?"

"Well..." Mama said, looking not so mad anymore.

"Never mind. I can tell by your tone that she hasn't. Do you think he would appreciate receiving her only to have her pass out within minutes of the first trial due to lack of food or a head injury?"

Mama's mouth opened and closed a couple times. "We feed her every once in a while! She ain't gonna *die*!"

"Right. I suppose next you'll tell me you feed her from each of the food groups."

"Of course not! But she does eat and gets the essential vitamins." Mama sounded like she was repeating something she'd read. Kind of like when I said my vocabulary words a bunch of times.

"Really? She gets all her 'essential vitamins' and doesn't eat from all the food groups? I'm curious. How do you manage that? MREs?"

I didn't know what MREs was, but Mama laughed like the fancy man had told a joke. "Well, I guess you could call it 'ready to eat'."

Mama held the door open for the fancy man to go inside. He stepped forward, grabbed the door and held it open, pointing at me then inside. I wasn't sure I wanted to go. Was it some kind of trick?

"Get your ass in here, Taryn!" Mama shouted. She turned and stomped inside.

The fancy man took one arm and put it across his waist, then leaned forward a little bit. "After you," he said, sounding super fancy.

Oh, that was fun! It was like he was telling me the same thing as Mama only in fancy words. I felt my mouth doing something funny. It was curling up at the edges. Oh, no! I didn't want the man to think I wanted to see him get hurt! I carefully edged around him, making sure not to touch him as I went inside.

Mama was meeting us at the door, pressing a small, empty can into the man's hands. Just the sight of it was making my belly grumble again. I knew what that was!

"What is this?" he asked, his eyes real big.

"It's what we feed her."

"This is cat food." He was making a disgust face. I knew what cats were. What I didn't know was why the fancy man didn't seem happy that it was for me, too. It was food. Wasn't it good to have food?

"I know what it is. It's what we feed her. It's cheap and, see right here? It has 'all essential vitamins'." Mama nodded firmly.

"For *cats*," the fancy man said.

"Vitamins is vitamins. It don't really matter as long as she gets 'em." Mama put her hands on her hips and stuck her chin out. "*And* they're only fifteen cents."

I thought the fancy man's eyes were going to pop out of his head. He closed his eyes and his hand went up to rub at the spot between them. Daddy came out from his room in just a pair of shorts. He walked into the kitchen and got one of his brown bottles of drink. I had tried a sip one time when I was really thirsty and had to wash the dishes, but it was super yuck!

"You're telling me," he began, pointing at Mama, "that you expect somebody to pay you to give your child up to an *experimental program* that has been surviving her whole life off of *cat food* and is being beaten on a regular basis? Is that what you're telling me right now, Mrs. Chambers? Mr. Chambers?"

His voice stayed quiet, but Mama was getting her angry face.

My eyes bounced back and forth between them. Daddy lifted his shoulders like he didn't really care about it.

"I don't see what the problem is," he told the fancy man.

"Yeah!" Mama seemed to be feeling even more brave now that Daddy was there. "We ain't asking for much. We just want a hand up outta this shit hole."

"I see," the fancy man murmured. Then he turned and put the full force of his gaze on me, which made Mama and Daddy look at me too. I didn't like everybody looking at me like that. "Hey, Taryn, may I get a picture of you real quick?"

A picture? Of me? Why was he asking? Mama and Daddy just usually did what they wanted. I had seen pictures on TV but I didn't know how they got on there. No matter what Mama and Daddy thought, I wasn't stupid. I didn't want anybody doing anything to me, so I shook my head back and forth, but I made sure to do it real slow in case his damage came back.

"What the hell do you mean 'no'?" Daddy snapped, moving toward me, but I was quick and jerked back and behind the couch.

The fancy man sighed. "That's enough. If you both would, please have a seat and allow me to speak to Taryn."

I was surprised that Mama and Daddy actually listened. They did not look happy. At all. But, they sat on the couch and waited for the fancy man. I did, too. Was he going to be angry that I didn't want him to take my picture? He didn't *look* angry, but I remembered how Mama smiled while she hurt me, so I knew that didn't mean he wouldn't hurt me.

He took a few steps away from Mama and Daddy and crouched down low to the floor. "Taryn, would you come speak to me, please?"

I wasn't sure I should. I didn't want to get too close and I was starting to think the damage in his brain had done something good for him because he was making Mama and Daddy do what he said. It made him seem...sneaky. That made *me* a little bit nervous.

"I promise I won't touch you," he added. I knew what 'promise' was, but nobody had ever promised me anything, so I wasn't sure I could believe that.

Still, I had a feeling the fancy man could wait there all day, so I slowly moved from behind the couch and walked a little bit closer to him, but not close enough that he could grab me. The corners of his eyes crinkled.

"Do you know what a picture is?" he asked.

I bobbed my head up and down, then looked real quick over to Mama and Daddy to make sure they weren't trying to sneak up on me.

"Okay. That's good. Do you know how a picture is taken?"

Slowly, I shook my head from side to side.

"How about if I show you and then you can decide if I can take your picture?"

"This is stupid," Mama grumbled.

I didn't look at her this time because the fancy man was pulling something out of his pocket. It looked like a tiny rectangle as long as his finger. It was a cell phone! I knew what it was because I'd heard the kids in our trailer park talking about them, but I had never seen one up close. I really wanted to touch it and see what it could do, but I didn't want to get close to the fancy man.

He pressed a button on the side, and it unfolded itself into a bigger, thinner rectangle with what looked like a tiny TV on it! Wow! I wanted to learn all about it, and my hands kept trying to reach out to touch it, so I pressed them tight together, only just then realizing I was still holding my treasures. What a great treasure that phone would be!

The fancy man pressed a button on it. I peered around to see, and the screen showed the living room! How was it doing that?? I must have asked that out loud, because the fancy man laughed and pressed another button, and suddenly I could see his face on the screen! My mouth dropped open.

Then he turned it around so it showed Mama's and Daddy's faces on the screen. He pressed another button and their faces froze on the screen.

"Did you see that? I just took a picture of your parents. It didn't hurt them at all! See?"

I looked back and forth from the screen to Mama and Daddy. They didn't seem bothered at all. Well, they still had their angry faces, but that was it. A little tremble of fear went through me when I saw their angry faces frozen on the screen. Then he did something else, pressed another button, and their picture was replaced by the fancy man's.

I studied his face. He didn't look like he was hurting. In fact, he was smiling, but I knew smiles were tricky so I didn't trust that and why would he be smiling anyway? He didn't make very much sense.

"Here's mine. It didn't hurt. It's easy and really fast. So, now may I take your picture?"

I thought about it. Even if it wouldn't hurt me, why would he want to take my picture?

"Oh my God! Just take the damn picture!" Daddy yelled, throwing his hands up.

The fancy man held his hand up in Daddy's direction, but he never looked away from me.

Then, he said something that made me really excited. "How about this, Taryn. If you let me take your picture, I'll take you to get something to eat. Anything you want."

"Just a damn minute! We didn't agree to that!" Mama snapped, leaning forward. I didn't look, though, because I was pretty sure the fancy man was in control.

"Pizza?" I asked, my eyes really big because I just couldn't believe it. I could finally try pizza??

The fancy man smiled. "Absolutely pizza. And a milkshake, too, if you want."

Wow!! But, wait...I looked down. I didn't think I could go anywhere in a bloody t-shirt. "I don't have anything appropriate to wear."

He didn't look bothered. "That's a big word! And you used it exactly right!" he said, then whispered, "Want to know a secret?"

Suddenly, I realized he was a lot closer than he used to be. When had that happened? I took a tiny step back and nodded my head. I *did* want to know his secret, especially the one that would make Mama and Daddy do what he said. That was a really important secret!

"I have some clothes that might fit you in my car. So we could go as soon as we're done if you want."

Oh. That wasn't so great of a secret. I had hoped it would be a better one, but it might be nice to have some other clothes. The ache that was always in my belly helped me make my decision.

"Okay," I said, but if he hurt me I was gonna...well...I didn't know exactly what I was gonna do, but I would do something!

The fancy man smiled and my body stepped back before I knew I was going to do it. He pressed a button on his screen. I braced myself, waiting for whatever was going to happen.

"All done!" Really? That was it? I hadn't felt anything at all! He didn't put his phone away, though. He kept pressing buttons, grabbed something from his tie, put it inside the phone, and kept tapping.

"What was that?" Daddy sounded super angry as he jumped up from the couch. I was back up against the wall before anybody even knew I was going to move. No way was I gonna be near Daddy when he was like that!

The fancy man didn't answer him. He just took a step to the side of the doorway. The next thing I knew, the door slammed open and a bunch of guys in all black clothes came storming in.

❧ 7 ❧

Mama let out a loud screech. I covered my ears with my treasures. I didn't know what was happening. Had the fancy man played a trick? I knew he was sneaky!! I got down on my knees and scooted behind the couch, keeping my treasures close. Leaning forward, I peeked around the edge of the couch.

"What is this?" Mama asked. One of the men in the black clothes had her arms behind her back and held her tight so she couldn't move. A teeny tiny part of me was glad she could know what it felt like to have somebody bigger making her be still. Another part of me was worried about what was going to happen. The fancy man pulled the bottom part of his suit jacket.

"This, Mrs. Chambers, is a team of government agents that is...off the books, for lack of a better phrase. They work for the government but aren't necessarily on the up-and-up." I didn't know what that meant. I wondered if he really knew what it meant either.

"Why are they *here?*" Daddy asked. "What's going on here?"

"Ahh, I've got a few minutes to spare. What's 'going on here' is that I spoke with my employer last evening when I walked out of this house. Upon speaking with him, he had decided that we were not going to be assisting you and would move on to better prospects."

"Then why – " The fancy man cut Mama right off.

"*However*, prior to my departure, I came across young Taryn outside." Mama and Daddy looked around for me. When they spotted me, their eyes were angry and promised lots more hurt. "I had a short conversation with her and realized she is far smarter than either one of you."

"Now *just a minute* – " Daddy didn't get to finish what he was going to say either.

"This six-year-old little girl is *so* resilient that she has managed to educate *herself*! She has figured out, despite having parents that abuse her, feed her cat food, and sit around drinking and doing drugs every day, how to gain access to educational materials. I discovered last night that she's intelligent *and* resourceful and upon speaking *for a second time* with my employer, he agreed that she likely only needs access to proper care to be able to thrive."

Mama and Daddy were silent as the fancy man paced back and forth. "He expressed to me this morning that he'd like me to return and procure the asset at any means necessary. Generally, this would be where I'd provide you with a check or a new home."

Daddy smiled, looking very pleased at hearing that.

"However, due to the condition she was in last night, her lack of records, and the fact that I just don't particularly care for either of you, I decided to go with our other method of asset procurement. And that is what leads us to now. In cases like yours, we make a record for Child Services with audio and visual records of abuse or neglect. Thank you for your statement by the way, Mrs. Chambers. Then, we arrange for an unfortunate incident to occur."

He waved his hand at the men in black that were in the

house. They had large red jugs filled with something that looked like water but smelled funny.

The fancy man pulled some things out of his pocket. He put one, a long white stick, in his mouth. The other thing was opened, he pulled out a little stick and did a magic trick! He swiped the stick across the paper and it lit up! He put it against the long white stick in his mouth then shook it and the fire went away! A thin stream of smoke floated in the air from the end of it. "When that is done, casualties are reported. A very sad affair to be sure. Of course, by the time the report is made, we've acquired our asset and no one is the wiser."

The men tipped up their jugs and they started splashing the liquid all over the floor. They were making a big mess! Mama and Daddy didn't like that at all! They started fighting to get away.

"You son of a bitch!" Daddy yelled right before one of the men punched him right in the face. Daddy fell on the floor, not moving. Strange little whimpering noises floated through the room. It sounded like a puppy somewhere. I kind of wanted to look for it, but I couldn't seem to move.

Another man lifted up a gun and hit Mama really hard in the head. It made a loud thunking noise and she fell down too. I just sat there, too scared to do anything. Was one of the men going to try to hit *me* next? I didn't like it when people hit me. My eyes burned but I wasn't going to let those stupid tears come. Not *ever* again! The fancy man went outside and the other men just moved through the house, down the hallway, splashing their stinky water all over the place.

The fancy man came back inside and got real close to where I was hiding behind the couch.

"Hey, Taryn," he said, real soft and quiet. "I brought you the clothes I told you about. Remember?"

I *did* remember he told me he had some clothes I could wear. Was he tricking me this time? Like he did Mama and Daddy? Because I was sure that was what had happened.

The fancy man opened the clothes up. There was a super pretty shirt with sparkles and lots of different colors on it and a fluffy skirt like I had seen some of the other girls wear when they went to the real school.

My hand reached up to touch it. I wondered what it felt like. Would the sparkles come off? I hoped not. Oh! I realized I had to put down my dolly, but I didn't want her to get lost, so I put her on my lap where she'd be safe. Then, looking from the clothes back to the fancy man, I took them, very carefully in case he was going to try to grab me, from his hand.

He didn't. "Why don't you go ahead and put those on?"

Did he think I was going to move from there? Go out to where all those strangers were with their stinky water? I did not think so! I really wanted to wear the pretty new clothes, but I didn't trust them. So, instead, I set my treasures on the floor, reached up and pulled on the back of the couch up at the top and used my feet to push hard as I could on the bottom part. The couch tilted backwards until the top part hit the wall, hiding me from the strangers.

I had done that before and Mama had gotten mad, saying that I was going to break the couch cause it was only fake wood and not real wood. I didn't think I was strong enough to break it, though.

I heard the fancy man laugh really loud when he saw what I had done. I didn't wait, I took the skirt and slid it on under my t-shirt. I found out it had shorts stuck to it underneath. How neat was that?! When my new skirt was on, I made a tent out of the shirt to hide in and put the other shirt on. It was a little bit hard to get it on because I wanted to make sure I could see the sparkles when I looked down. It was super pretty. I liked it a lot. I had never had anything pretty before. When I was all finished, I grabbed my treasures and crawled to the end of the couch, peeking out at the strangers. They were all waiting, standing there staring right where I peeked out from.

They were being really weird.

The fancy man crouched down, too close to the couch for me! "All done?"

I nodded. Did he want me to come out? I wasn't sure I wanted to do that. Then again...they weren't doing any more hitting and Mama and Daddy for sure couldn't get me.

"Are you ready to go get that pizza?" he asked.

My eyes got bigger. I had almost forgot about that! When I saw he had tricked Mama and Daddy, I thought he'd been tricking me about the pizza, too! I wondered if he really was tricking me just to get me to come out from behind the couch. Then I looked at all the strangers. They looked like they had big muscles and could probably just move the couch if they wanted.

I looked at the fancy man. He was still too close. If I went out there, he'd be able to touch me and I really didn't want that. How should I tell him to go away? Oh! I knew!

I nodded my head to let the fancy man know I was ready if he was really going to take me to find pizza. I set Baby Bear on the floor so my hand was free then used that hand to make the 'shoo' motion. People did that when bugs got in their faces. Daddy did that to me when I was 'bugging' him, so I thought that was the right thing to do.

The fancy man laughed real quiet and the strangers laughed too, but he did what I wanted him to do so I guessed I was right. He took three giant steps back which almost made him bump into one of the strangers. I checked to make sure the strangers weren't too close before I got Baby Bear and crawled out from behind the couch.

I squeezed tight to my treasures in case any of the strangers wanted to take them away. Mama and Daddy were still on the floor. They didn't move at all when the strangers stepped over them. I did *not* think that was a good time to take a nap!

The fancy man looked me over. "Ahh. Shoes," he murmured. "We'll need some. Any in the rooms back there?"

I didn't think he was talking to me. He wasn't looking at me. He was looking at one of the strangers. The stranger went down the hallway and I heard doors opening and closing. Their stinky water was starting to make me feel sick. Long minutes went by until the stranger came back, shaking his head.

The fancy man looked like he was trying real hard not to get an angry face. "Can someone please go find the child some shoes?"

Some of them turned to leave but then one turned back around. "Uh...what size, Mr. Bennett?"

The fancy man looked at my feet then back at the stranger. "Whatever size you think will fit. She's pretty small. Just get several options." He pulled his phone out, pressing some more buttons. We waited. I stood there and the fancy man did stuff on his phone. Some of the strangers took Mama and Daddy back down the hallway. I was glad they were sleeping so they wouldn't get hit anymore. It was *not* fun to be hit.

Footsteps on the porch had me looking to see the other strangers coming back. They all had lots of shoes and sizes. There were girl shoes and boy shoes. Wow! They were fast. Where did they get all of those shoes?

They all started to come towards me, but my body was already moving backwards. I never even thought about moving. It just happened. The fancy man held up a fist and they all stopped. I did not like seeing that fist. Fists were bad. They hurt a lot. He put his fist down, took a pair of the shoes from one of the strangers, and rolled them across the floor to me.

I sat down on the floor and slipped them on. My foot slid around inside but since I couldn't remember ever actually wearing shoes, I wasn't sure what they were supposed to feel like. I stood up, my toes curling like they were fingers trying to hold onto the shoes. I went to take a step and my foot came right out. I looked at it in surprise. I hadn't expected that to happen!

"Not those," the fancy man said.

I sat back down, took them off, and rolled them back to him. That was a fun part. I liked rolling the shoes. That's how it went for a while. He would take some shoes from one of the strangers, roll them to me, I would put them on, he would say no and I would roll them back. Finally, I got to a pair of shoes, and he said, "Those will do."

I was glad he said that because I liked those shoes. They were called sandals and just had straps on them. I had a hard time figuring out the straps and the fancy man had wanted to help me but I didn't want him to get close, so he had just told me things like 'other one', or 'send it across your foot' to help me figure it out.

It was funny, though, because I had seen one of the neighbor girls wearing some just like those! I had liked them then, but I really liked to see them on my own feet. I felt bad that I was getting blood on all the shoes, but the fancy man had told me not to worry about it. Maybe he was going to wipe them off or just throw the shoes away.

The fancy man pointed to the door and all of the strangers started to leave. Were they coming with us to get the pizza? I didn't know if I liked that idea. There were a lot of them and they were pretty big. What if they ate it all?

"Ready?" the fancy man asked me.

I nodded. I was ready for pizza, but I looked back at the hallway. I hoped they wouldn't be too mad at me when I got back. I didn't want them to hurt me again. Still, the thought of pizza was too much to make me stay, so when the fancy man went to the door, I followed him.

He held the door open again. "After you," he told me.

A small smile curled my lips as I edged past him, very careful not to touch him. We got to the bottom of the steps and all the strangers started disappearing! I thought they must be magic or something to be able to do that! They were super sneaky!

The fancy man suddenly got my attention. He pulled out the paper and sticks he'd had earlier.

"Watch this," he said. Then he took one of the sticks and brushed it hard across the paper. It lit up!

"Wow," I said, moving both my treasures to one hand and reaching up with the other to touch it.

"Careful! That's hot," he warned. Right. I knew that. I had just forgotten. But then he held it out for me, showing where to grab it so I could hold it. I was excited. It reminded me of some of the things the other kids would play with sometimes. They would run around with a little stick and it would have sparkles on the end of it. This one didn't have sparkles but it was still pretty. I watched the flame dance around on the end of the stick.

"Silly me," the fancy man said. "We can't take that in the car. Why don't you throw it away...hmm...maybe over there by your steps so we don't catch the grass on fire. Oh, and I brought you something."

The fancy man didn't really give me any time to think. He just kept talking and then...*then* he did something really neat. He reached into his jacket pocket and pulled out one of the most beautiful dolls I had ever seen. It was a fairy doll with wings and sparkles and it was so pretty and looked so soft I just wanted to hug her right then! I reached up, forgetting about the fire stick.

"Careful," the fancy man warned, pulling the doll back.

That was right! He'd told me to throw it away. I turned just enough to see the steps where he'd said it should go, and barely paid attention as I threw it before turning back to grab the doll before he decided to take it away.

A loud *whoosh* went up behind me and my back heated up just as my tiny hand wrapped around the doll. I moved to turn around, because I hadn't heard that sound before, but the fancy man was blocking me. He had gotten too close, so I moved faster toward his car to keep him from touching me. Before I knew it, we were in the car and I was introducing my new doll to my other treasures. I thought they were all as excited to try the pizza as I was.

It didn't take us very long to get there at all. I was so excited! I had never been to eat at a restaurant before. It was so fun and there were so many choices. The fancy man helped me order. There was a weird part where a lady asked what had happened to my head, but the fancy man said I liked to pretend every day was Halloween. I didn't know what he meant by that but when the lady looked at me, I just waved, which had seemed to work on that Katie girl, and she showed us where we could sit.

We got to sit in a quiet corner by a window in a real, actual booth! The fancy man seemed to be watching for something. It wasn't until some firetrucks went by with their really loud sirens that he looked back at me and smiled. And it was not a nice smile. It was one that gave me shivers but by then I was too busy filling my belly up with the pizza to be too worried about it right then. It was so good I wanted to eat it every day!

8

I was for sure. Pizza was my new favorite food. Of course, pizza was the only other food I'd ever had aside from what Mama gave me sometimes. Pizza was *way* better than that even if I did burn my mouth on it. I had never had food that came out of the oven. I could see why Mama and Daddy liked to eat that instead of what they gave me.

When we were all finished, we got back in the fancy man's car. I got to sit in the front, but I still couldn't see much over the top. From my window, I could see lots and lots of buildings. Way more than near our trailer.

I thought he was going to take me back to the trailer, and that made me kind of worried because I just *knew* they were gonna be really mad that I had had pizza. We drove for a lot longer than it took us to get to the pizza place and I didn't recognize any of the things we had passed on the way to get there.

That was about the time I started to wonder what the fancy man was doing. It was starting to feel a lot like that First Forty-Eight show. Was the fancy man 'kidnapping' me? I had thought if that ever happened to me, I'd be really scared and sad like on the TV shows I saw sometimes, but I wasn't as sad as I thought I'd be. I think, maybe, because he had given me some food. I was starting to feel a pressure in my belly.

Finally, my curiosity got the best of me and I asked, "Where are we going?"

The fancy man took a quick look over his shoulder at me. "What makes you think I'm not taking you home?"

Knowing he couldn't see me, I decided to try the neat thing he did with his eyes to Mama. I don't think it worked very well though, because I just ended up being able to see my nose. "I 'straplated," I told him, using my new big word.

He looked over at me again, his eyebrows pulled in. "You...what?"

I sighed real big. He must be having a hard time with his damage again. So, real slow, I said, "I. Straaa. Plaaaayyyyyy. Teeeddddd."

He still looked like he was having a hard time, so I added, "It's a big word. It means when I make a guess cuz of the evdens."

The corners of the fancy man's eyes crinkled and he let out a small laugh. The sound made me jerk back a little. Seeing that, he pressed his lips into a straight line. "A big word that means making a guess because of the...eh-vi-dence? You mean ex-trap-o-late?"

I sighed again, crossing my arms like Mama does. It felt weird to do that, so I dropped them down again. Why was he saying his words slow? Did he think I was dumb? *I* wasn't the one with the damage! "I said that, right?" I asked, because I suddenly wasn't so sure if he had to ask me if that's what I meant. And plus, it *did* sound a little different when he said it.

He smiled again. "Right. Well, Taryn, I'm going to be honest with you, okay?"

I nodded. Of course, I wanted him to be honest. I knew that meant telling the truth.

"Your Mama and Daddy...well, they tried to make a deal...," he seemed unsure what to say next.

I wasn't stupid. "You mean they sold me." That was part of goods and services. The video said when you gave something for money or trade, it was selling.

The fancy man looked really surprised. His eyebrows went way up high. "Well, yes. They did. And what that means for you, is that you get to go stay at a really nice place where you can have a safe place to sleep every night, and a bath, and clean clothes."

I wasn't sure what a bath was, but I was thinking it was a sneaky way of saying a shower. I didn't want anything to do with that! Clean clothes were okay, but I had some pretty ones so I didn't really need any new ones. I usually had a safe place to sleep. Under the porch with the kitties. It didn't sound like it was much different from what I did before.

I started to wiggle in my seat. I think I'd had too much drink. I really had to go, but I didn't see any trees anywhere.

"What are you doing?" the fancy man sounded worried. "Do you need the restroom?"

What's a restroom? A place for a rest? A nap room? I shook my head, still squirming in my seat. I didn't need a nap! I had to pee!

The fancy man didn't look like he believed me. He sighed. After a few minutes, he pulled over to a building that had lots of cars and trucks of all different colors around it. Wow! "Come on," he said. "We need to do something about your hair anyway. Leave your toys here. They'll be safe and you shouldn't bring them in the store or they might think you're trying to steal them and take them away. If you want, you can put them under your seat."

He got out of his car and came around to my side as I hid my treasures, whispering that I'd be back for them, and climbed out. I pushed the door closed and his hand reached out, but I was already out of the way. Had he been going to touch me? My face scrunched up at him. He looked down at me, then his hand, then he let it drop back down to his side. "Stay close."

My nose wrinkled. I didn't want to stay close to him. He started walking slowly toward the store, looking back over his shoulder at me to make sure I was coming. I started to follow after him. I had never been in a store before. I was excited to see what was in there! I kept looking around as we walked. There were so many people and colors and cars and everything was moving around. It was a lot!

"Taryn!" the fancy man yelled really loud, making me freeze in my spot. I looked to where his voice came from only to see a big, gray car slamming to a stop inches from me. Where had it come from?! My eyes were huge and it felt like my heart had stopped right inside my chest!

Then, the fancy man was there, his hands were on my shoulders, and he was talking really fast. It took a minute for my brain to catch up to what was happening. It had happened so fast!

"...are you okay? Are you hurt? Taryn?" I looked from him back to the car that was still *right there*. I could almost feel it rumbling like it wanted to get me. I felt my eyes burn and the tears well up because it had scared me.

"Taryn," the firm voice of the fancy man had me looking back at him. "Did the car hit you?"

My mouth dropped open. Cars could *hit* people? How? With what? They didn't have hands...or *did* they? I shook my head then looked back at the car, trying to figure out where its hands would be. Did it hit with its doors? But, no. Those weren't near me. Maybe its wheels? I shook my head again. It hadn't hit me.

The fancy man let out a big whoosh of air, then stood back up so he was beside me.

"Oh my God! Did I hit her?! She's bleeding!! Oh my God! I'm so sorry, sweetie! I didn't see you! Oh my God! Did you call an ambulance?!" a woman's high pitched voice came from nearby.

"No, no, no!" the fancy man said. Then he laughed a little. "It's fake blood. She loves Halloween and was trying out some new makeup at home. She's big into zombies right now."

One hand stayed on my shoulder, not squeezing or hurting, just staying there. The heavy weight of it starting to make my skin itchy.

"Really?" The woman came close, but I moved quick, backing up around the fancy man. His hand fell from my shoulder.

"Taryn," he said, edging a little sideways so the woman could see me, "can you let the nice lady know you're all right?"

How did he know she was a nice lady? I didn't know her at all. I looked up at the fancy man. "She's a stranger," I told him, very seriously.

At hearing me speak, the woman let out a weak laugh. "That I am. So, you don't have to talk to me. You can just nod yes or no. Are you okay?"

I nodded.

"Did I bump you with my car?"

I shook my head and the lady looked like she was going to fall down, leaning against the car, and letting out a big breath of air. "Oh, thank God!" Then she looked at me again. "You should really watch where you're going."

That didn't make sense to me. She was the one that almost bumped me with her car. It seemed like she should be the one watching where she was going. I may not have known all the rules, but I did know that people were smaller than cars and the car was supposed to be careful of the people, not the other way around. Stranger or not, she needed to know she was wrong.

"Bein' that your car is bigger than me, and the police say 'destrians have the 'right of way', I think that means maybe you should be more careful. What if I was a baby? Cars are sposed to have things called safety features that 'lert the driver so they know something is there before the car even moves. That means you didn't listen to the 'lert or you need to fix it. It's illegal to drive with broke safety features."

The woman's mouth had dropped open while I talked to her. I didn't think she liked what I had said, because she was starting to get an angry face. She gave me a mean look.

The fancy man laughed, "You're absolutely right, Taryn." Then he turned to the woman. "You know, there's a minimum one year sentence for operating a motor vehicle with a broken alert system. In fact, ninety percent of vehicles nowadays have automatic braking for anything within a certain distance of the vehicle. It seems either you were trying to run her over, or you've got a faulty system. Add in the automatic reporting system and I'm fairly certain this incident has already been recorded from your vehicle and sent to the appropriate authorities. I'm sure the camera feed from the store can corroborate should you attempt —"

"What do you want?" the woman asked, tears at the corners of her eyes. Why was she sad?

"Why, nothing," the fancy man said with a mean smile. It was a smile like Mama and Daddy had. "Except for you to get your motor vehicle's alert system fixed. Have a good day, Ma'am."

Then he turned to leave, holding his hand out to me. I didn't want to touch him. Not at all. *But*, I didn't want another car trying to smack me either. So, I reached one shaking hand up and grabbed hold of his smallest finger. Why was I shaking? I hadn't even noticed.

The fancy man started walking again and I let his arm stretch out before I followed, making sure there was lots of space. We made it all the way to the door without any more cars trying to hit me.

The doors opened and we stepped into a tiny clear room.

"Welcome to your local neighborhood Family Mart Express. Please select your destination." I looked around, trying to see who else was there, but there wasn't anybody! The fancy man started pressing things on a screen stuck on one of the walls, then we were moving. The whole tiny room was moving! And I stumbled, placing one hand on the wall, not expecting that to happen. The fancy man let out a little laugh, curling his finger to wrap around the edge of my hand. I looked around and could see people in other tiny, clear rooms that were being moved all around the big store, too.

He turned us around so we were facing the opening. It stopped and the fancy man stepped out to get something. When he got back in, the room said, "I detect that you've chosen. Shampoo. For Children. Strawberry scented. If this is correct, please scan your card to purchase your items."

My mouth dropped open and my eyes got really big as the fancy man held up a tiny triangle to the screen in the room. The screen flashed green and the room moved again. Wow! We stopped a few more times and each time, he held up his little triangle. I wondered where I could get a triangle, if it let you get whatever you wanted!

Finally, we stopped in front of a door. It slid open and the fancy man did his funny bow to me and said, "After you."

❧ 9 ❧

My lips curled up at the corners at the way he did that. I went through the doorway to see a bathroom. Only, there was no shower. Just a toilet and a sink. Huh. I had never used a toilet before. We had one at our house, but I never got to use it because Mama and Daddy didn't like me being in the house anyway.

"All right, Taryn," the fancy man had followed me into the bathroom and turned so his back was to me. Then he pulled down a little table from the wall. "Why don't you try to use the toilet and I'll get some of this stuff set up so we can clean you up a bit."

Hmm...okay. I guessed I would try. Without further ado, I dropped my new fluffy skirt and climbed onto the toilet. My belly felt so much better when I was done. I started to hop down but the fancy man said, "Don't forget to wipe."

Wipe what? What was he talking about now? When he didn't hear me moving, he added, "With toilet paper. It's over on the wall. Pull some off and clean off any extra..." He trailed off, not saying anything else. I saw the paper he was talking about. I reached over to 'pull some off' and it just kept coming and coming. Soon, I had a pile of it at my feet.

That was when I saw there were little squares and not just one big piece, so I took it in both hands and ripped it apart. I had three squares. I wasn't sure what I was supposed to 'wipe', so I just wiped everything from my belly on down to my knees and everywhere in between. Then I jumped off, my sandals making a tapping noise when they hit the floor, and pulled up my fluffy skirt.

"Wash your hands," the fancy man said quietly.

Hmm...that was new. Wash my hands? I didn't think he wanted me to take a shower. There wasn't one in there and I didn't want to anyway. Not hearing me move, he turned around and pointed at the sink. I walked to it but wasn't quite sure what else was expected. Did he just want me to rinse them off? Or did he want me to scrub them like I did the dishes? There was nothing to scrub with, though.

The fancy man came closer to me. He put his hand under the stick in the wall and water came out, pouring into the sink. Then he put his hand under another stick and a thick liquid came out onto his hand. He scrubbed them together and put them back under the water stick.

"Move your hands this way to make the water hotter," his hands moved closer toward me, then he moved them to the other side, "and this way to make the water colder."

Wow! I had been watching real close, so when he moved his hand under a blue light on the wall, and the water went away, I started doing just like he did. Water was so nice when it was warm and not super cold!

When I finally got done, he told me, "I'm going to need you to sit up here so I can clean you up some." I couldn't get up there. It was too high. Still, I grabbed the edge and hopped a couple times, trying to pull myself up and over. It didn't work. I looked at the fancy man and he said, "I could help you."

Help me? I couldn't remember that ever happening before. How would he help me? Helping was supposed to be a good thing. I nodded, so he'd know I was going to let him try with the helping.

Very slowly, his hands moved towards me. I watched them carefully, hoping he wasn't going to hurt me. Still super slow, they wrapped around my waist, making my whole body go stiff, and I was lifted up off my feet, turned around and my butt landed on the table. I didn't relax until he took his hands away again.

The next few minutes were not fun because the fancy man had to put stuff on my head, knees, and feet to 'kill the germs'. I didn't know what he meant by that and was a little worried he was killing something on me that needed to be there. I knew killing wasn't good. After he did that, he put colorful sticky things on them.

Then he had me lay down with my head waaayyy far back so it went over the sink. Water turned on and I got really scared then because I thought he was going to hold me under there like Mama did, and I wanted to breathe! Tiny noises started coming from my throat. I wanted them to stop because I didn't want to make the fancy man angry, but I couldn't!

My eyes squeezed shut tight and I sucked in big gulps of air. My fingers started to hurt and I thought I was probably squeezing something too tight.

The fancy man just made "shhhh" noises at me and moved his hands faster on my hair.

The next thing I knew, I opened my eyes, and I was sitting on the floor with my back against the wall. My knees were pulled up tight to my chest and the fancy man was crouched down a little ways away from me. There was wet on my face and I got mad at myself because I knew I had cried again.

My hair was wet on my back. The water from it was soaking through my shirt. When I looked at the fancy man, he gave me a little smile.

"There we are. Are you ready to go find that milkshake?" His voice was super soft and quiet. He didn't sound angry at all. He handed me a ball of the white paper, making a motion like he was wiping his face. I thought that must be what he wanted me to do, so I used the paper to scrub my face clean.

I still wasn't sure about the milkshake, but I was for sure ready to go! I nodded and got to my feet. My legs felt shaky, like they wanted me to sit back down, but I didn't. I wanted to get out of there.

The fancy man led me back out to the tiny, clear room and it took us back to the spot where we had come in. The fancy man started walking back across the big gray space filled with cars and trucks, but I didn't follow him. I remembered what happened last time. After a few steps, he turned to look at me. I stayed in my spot but held up my hand. The fancy man looked surprised, but he still smiled at me. I decided I really didn't like it when people smiled at me.

He came back and held his hand out. I wrapped my fingers around his smallest one like last time and let his arm stretch waaayyy out before I followed him back to the car. He drove for a little while then went through something he called a 'drive through'. We pulled up to a big box and he pressed buttons on it, waved his little triangle, and then there was a lot of different noises before a smaller box unfolded from the bigger box. The smaller box had drinks in it! Wow!

The fancy man handed one to me and it was cold when I touched it. It had a stick poking out of the top and I watched him closely to see what he did. He put the stick in his mouth. That was weird, but, okay I would try it.

I put the stick in my mouth, but it didn't do anything! I looked at the stick. Was it broken? I didn't want the broken one! I looked back at the man. He had a little smile again. Reaching over, he took the little stick away, and took the top off of my cup. Cold air came up to my face when I lifted it.

I dipped my tongue in and my eyes almost popped out of my head because it was soooo yum! Why would people drink anything else? It was even better than pizza! I tipped the cup up and then knew I shouldn't have done that because the whole thing inside slid down and plopped right onto my face. It was cold and I couldn't breathe! I pulled it back super quick and took a big breath.

I looked at the fancy man. He was laughing, his shoulders shaking. He picked up some white paper and reached over, wiping at my face. I looked at the 'milkshake', wondering why it had done that to me. Then the fancy man handed me a spoon. That was a lot better. I ate some of it but couldn't eat much because my belly felt too full from the few bites of pizza and the milkshake. It wasn't used to having so much in there.

I leaned back on my seat, cuddling my treasures, and the fancy man pushed a button, making music play in the car. Before I knew it, I was falling asleep, tired cause of all the new stuff I got to do.

When I woke up, it was dark outside. I didn't know how long we'd been in the car for, but the car was moving slow. I looked over to the fancy man, watching him push buttons on the screen. After a minute, he looked over and saw that I was awake.

"We're here," he told me, but I didn't see anything except darkness and a super big fence. As the car got closer, the fence opened up and we went right on through. The car stayed on a path that took us straight up to a big, big building. It was even bigger than the last one.

There were some people standing outside. Were they waiting for us? A big sign was at the top of the doors. I sounded them out. "Vic-tor-i-ous Lab-or-a-tor-ies. Victorious Laboratories. What's that?"

The fancy man looked happy that I asked. "*That* is your new home."

The car stopped and he opened up his door. "Come on."

Already, my door was being opened. Hands were reaching in. They were going to touch me. They were going to hurt me! A loud scream came out of my throat. I didn't know I could make that sound!

The fancy man was saying something to the people at my door, but I didn't really listen to him because I was trying to climb over the seat and get away from them. I slid onto the floor in the back of the car, holding tight to my treasures as my breath came in big gasps.

The back door opened and I jerked away from it. "Taryn." It was the fancy man. I looked up at him, trying to stop shaking. "I'm sorry. I forgot to warn them. You can come out now. They won't touch you."

I wasn't so sure about that. "It's all right. Come on. Don't you want to see your new home?"

Well...not if people were going to be touching me. I stayed there, then he did something that made me feel a lot better. He stepped back, pulling the car door wide open, bowed, and said in his super fancy voice, "After you."

My lips did that twisty thing and I slowly crawled out of the car, peeking around the door to make sure nobody was hiding to grab me. Lots of them had white jackets on but they had all backed away. Everyone was looking at me. I didn't like that, so I ducked my head, my long white hair falling down by my face. That's when I saw the ground was gray. Just like at the other building; the store. I didn't see any other cars here, but I hadn't seen the one that tried to smack me either.

The fancy man had already closed the door and crossed over to the door where all the other people were waiting. I just stood there. I knew what it meant when the ground was gray. One of the people in white said something to him and he turned around. He looked confused for a minute, then he came back. His arm stretched way out and I moved all three of my treasures to hold in one arm. Then I reached up with my free hand and wrapped all my fingers around his smallest one so he could lead me inside to my new home.

ONE MONTH LATER...

I hated this place. I wanted to go back to Mama and Daddy. The fancy man had brought me here, showed me my new 'room', and left. I hadn't seen him again. My room had a bed, which I didn't sleep on because I was so used to sleeping on the ground, a toilet, a sink, and walls. One wall was glass and a piece of it lifted up to let people in and out.

The first day was okay. I had been shown my room, I got to keep my treasures, they gave me food, and they left me alone. The second day was when I realized how bad I had messed up going with the stranger. The fancy man. I was so angry with him.

The people in the white coats had come to me. They started sticking me with needles. They didn't care that I didn't want them to do it. They did it anyway. My blood went out and other stuff went in. Sometimes the stuff they put in me was clear, sometimes it was other colors.

No matter what color it was, it always, *always* made me sick. I had never felt this bad before. I got food but I couldn't keep it in my body. I stayed on the floor near the toilet in my room, throwing up even when I didn't eat anything. I felt tired all the time, barely able to hold myself up enough to get my head over the toilet bowl. I thought they were killing me with their colored waters.

It had been weeks of them sticking me with their needles and cutting off pieces of my skin. I didn't know how much more I could take. The worst part was that I knew I wasn't the only one. There were other kids there. I heard them crying. Screaming. Begging to go home.

When I'd heard it the first night, I couldn't figure out why they would want that. Then I knew. I felt the fire going into my body when they put their colored water in the needles. The fire burned me from the inside out. Nothing I could do made it stop. Then, I was screaming my pain right along with the other kids.

I didn't know why the people in the white coats were doing that to us. Until I did. I knew the days because each time they took me into their 'treatment' room, one of the white coats would say something like "Taryn Chambers. Day 6. Trial seven three two," then they would stick me with their needles again.

So I knew, on Day 8, what they were trying to do because that day, I woke up in more pain than each other day. My fingers hurt to even have the sheet touching them. It felt like my finger bones were growing and it hurt so bad. Even though the tears tried to come and my eyes burned, I wouldn't cry.

Small whimpering sounds came out of my throat. I squeezed and pressed on my fingers, trying to make the pain stop. Then, I pressed right there at the bend near the very tip of my finger and fire went through it.

Underneath my normal fingernail, something pointy and white pushed through my skin leaving the tip of my finger covered in blood. It wasn't another fingernail. It was curved and sharp at the end. I wasn't sure what they had done to me or why they had done it but I knew they had made me different.

They had changed me.

The End

(Continue Taryn's story in Book 1 of the Changed series.)

ABOUT THE AUTHOR

Hi, my name is Christina Lanier. Thanks so much for reading and getting to know Taryn. If you enjoyed this novella of the Changed series, please go online and leave a review. I'm also author of the Slated series. I live on the Atlantic coast, have 4 kids, and enjoy sharing my stories with the world. You can follow me on Facebook: @christinalanierauthor, or visit my website at www.christinalanier.com.

www.ingramcontent.com/pod-product-compliance
Lightning Source LLC
Chambersburg PA
CBHW021343060726
47591CB00006B/2144